AN UNEXPECTED NOTIFICATION
By
REDA SHAHID

Reda Shahid was born and brought up in Calcutta, India. She lives in Lucknow with her family, where she has completed her education. She is an MBA, orator and writer. Reda has been associated with brands like Radio Mirchi (Outdoor Broadcasting Jock) and Business Standard Newspaper (Campus Reporter).

Moreover, often, she writes poetries, write-ups and stories. She says she likes to travel and live in her solitude at times as it let her express her thoughts and emotions. She loves nature and likes to observe it. "An Unexpected Notification" is her debut novelette, which gives a message that the universe does respond to one's wishes and how a person can help you discover the purpose of your life. She has a belief that if her writing can heal someone or help them do better at life, she would consider herself a successful writer.

To know more about her, you can connect with her on www.redashahid.com or follow her on Instagram: redashahid Facebook: redashahidofficial Twitter: RedaShahid

An Unexpected Notification

(From Social Media Crush to Life Purpose)

REDA SHAHID

wovenwordspublishers
.com

Woven Words Publishers OPC Pvt. Ltd.

Registered Office:

Vill: Raipur, P.O: Raipur Paschimbar,

Dist: Purba Midnapore, Pin: 721401,

West Bengal, India.

Branch Office(Operations): Hyderabad

www.wovenwordspublishers.com

Email: publish@wovenwordspublishers.com

First published by Woven Words Publishers OPC Pvt. Ltd., 2019

Copyright© Reda Shahid, 2019

NOVEL

IMPRINT: WOVEN WORDS LAUNCHPAD

ISBN 13: 978-9388762113

ISBN 10: 9388762118

Price: $ 6/₹500

Printed and bound in India by Woven Words Publishers

To,

Both my grandfathers Late Mr Abdul Waheed (Paternal) &
Late Dr Malikzada Manzoor Ahmed(Maternal)

Contents

Acknowledgement

'Is Kahani ko kitaab banane ke peeche bohat logo ka haath hai.'

I want to express my sincere gratitude firstly to ALLAH for making my dream come true, and my parents without whom the book and I both wouldn't have existed.

A legendary name is already associated with me Late Dr Malikzada Manzoor Ahmed, I want to thank you, Nana, for passing on your blessings, interest and fondness towards literature in me. I promise I will never let you down.

I can't thank my mother, my best friend, Mrs Huma Shahid enough for all that she has done for me. She is the most beautiful soul and face that exists in the world for me. I haven't seen anyone like her. My first yet most interested audience, showing interest in every line that I kept on adding and asking me about the updates. It increased my morale and courage to continue writing. Thank You so much, Mumma!

Secondly, a big big thank you to my superhero, my mentor, my lifeline my dad Mr Shahid Waheed whom I lovingly call 'Papuu.' The man who has set a benchmark in my life, the classiest man I know. What people say is correct - 'Behind every successful woman there is a man.' I want to improvise it 'behind every successful daughter is a father.' Thank you, Papa, for always showing trust in me, believing in my potential and making me an independent girl. You have always given me space and freedom to make my own decisions and follow my own choices rather than imposing yours upon me. It takes anyone to be a father, but thank you for being my Papu, more than a father. You are not just a father but a father figure, the one I can always count on, seek advice and guidance from.

I cannot afford to forget thanking my biggest support, my partner in crime, my big brother BHAI, Mr Faraz Shahid. The man who has always been there for me, helping me deciding the names of my characters and giving me some of the weirdest suggestions that added fun to my journey of writing. Bhai, without you, I couldn't have promoted my book. Thank you for being so supportive, caring and loving. Also, I would like to thank my sis-in-law Mrs Hera Faraz for being supportive in the making of this book.

Next, I would like to thank both my uncles Mr Jawaid Malikzada and Mr Parvez Mehmood for being humble and helping me spread the word about my book.

Moreover, I would like to thank my publisher Mr Mosiur Rehman and team from the bottom of my heart for being so supportive and co-operative all through the publishing process. He gave his valuable suggestions yet letting me have the last words. Also, I would like to thank my teacher Mrs Deepika Punjabi who discovered the hidden talent in me and encouraged me to write. Last but not least, I want to thank myself for not giving up on the story and re-writing the book once again all from scratch when I have lost my manuscript and I couldn't end up my acknowledgement without thanking Haana & Sikander for redefining our definition of Love.

A very big thanks to all my readers for believing in the story and reading my book.

Once in your life-time, the universe sends a person to change your life,

They are not always Love but Crush,

For Better or Worse?

Haana-An Ambitious Girl

*Hello! I am Haana, 21 years old girl from Delhi. I am an
ambitious girl. I was enjoying my single-hood when I realised
I had a crush on a guy named Sikander, but I don't know
whether he likes me back or not?*

Sikander- The Social Media Swagger

Hi, my fans! As you all know, I am Sikander, 30 years old business tycoon. They call me a 'Social Media Swagger.' I am rich, handsome, popular; you can call me a 'Man of your Dreams.' I was living a healthy life when something happened, and my life was changed. But what was such that occurred?

1

Crossed Paths

AUGUST 29, 2016 7:45 PM

It was quarter-to-eight. Haana was home that evening with her mom and was about to put her clothes into the washing machine when her phone rang and one of her friends, Kavya, proposed if she would like to hang out with her. She was not very sure whether to agree and go out with her or stay home and wash her dirty clothes but, eventually, she went out, leaving the task which she thought was boring and could be done later.

Kavya was on her way to Haana's place, who managed to get ready within five minutes without dressing properly as she decided not to change because it would take a lot of time and they not allowed to stay out late. To look presentable, she applied foundation and highlighted the best part of her face i.e. eyes with kohl. For a change, she wore big round earrings. She had short wavy hair so she didn't have options to experiment much with them.

At 8 pm they were in the car, meanwhile, she thought 'what if I meet the love of my life today?' She had no idea all these thoughts would ever come into manifestation or there was a force that made her thought so. It was ten-past-eight, they reached Cafe Bronze, a popular cafe in Delhi. As they entered the rooftop, right next to the pillar, was a place for four where they both settled. Meanwhile, Kavya was busy clicking selfies and Haana had no idea what to do exactly. She was wondering, "Ye khud-pasand ladki sirf apne tasveer he kyu kheech rahe hai"? (Why is this self-obsessed girl only clicking her pictures?)

She quietly sat down looking at the pillar rather than looking here and there. Kavya asked her to come and sit beside her, to which, Haana thought Kavya must be assuming her to be left alone while she was busy clicking selfies. So, she took the seat beside Kavya.

"Hi let's take a selfie."

Haana was expecting those words from her, but she was hardly concerned. Instead of asking her for a photograph together, now she was busy checking in. Haana wondered who would be interested in knowing where she was. As far as her parents knew she was with her, or maybe some other concerned people. All she was wondering was why had she asked her to join her when she had to show the world that she was enjoying her solo time.

Being girls of the 21st century, they had all the rights to discuss guys. It was when Haana told Kavya that the place was not much happening, Kavya interrupted her, saying, "Look, the guys at the table next to the pillar are all looking this way."

After a pause of few seconds, Haana too looked in the same direction to confirm whether Kavya was right and if she was, then whether those guys were good enough to even stare at them. Haana glimpsed there and found it to be a group, if not a gang of men, because all of them seemed to be above 30 years old, except one guy who was busy on-call and looked very tensed and disturbed. Haana's picky nature did not allow her to look into other qualities as she brushed her vision quickly in the opposite direction to make sure she's not stared at by any member of that gang.

Haana was a very-hard-to-please type of girl. For her, the most handsome boy of her college even didn't qualify for her attention. She would give heed to other things but not boys like she was then pondering over her glass of chocolate shake which she had to finish soon because she wanted to leave. But Kavya insisted her to stay for some time more. It was eight-twenty (Haana had started countdown by then) when Kavya repeated the same words-"Look! They are looking at us again."

Haana's irritation had crossed all boundaries of being patient, on hearing Kavya's comment. She was not sure why would Kavya even look at that 30-year-old club. She assumed, either Kavya was interested in any of those guys or she was trying to seek the attention of those who could be called 'uncles.' Anyways, Haana was not interested in them. Kavya realised Haana's annoyance and changed the topic. Haana's eyes brushed aside a tall, muscular, not so dark and handsome guy who passed by. He was the same guy who looked disturbed when talking on the phone. Haana glanced at him and found him an average handsome guy (an average handsome is Haana's definition of describing guys who are not extraordinarily handsome but they are good looking, tough and wow!)
Haana joked about him to Kavya saying-
"Lagta hai is ladke ne Kuch zyada he protein shake pee lia" (Seems like this guy has consumed a lot of protein shake.)
They laughed not on him but on her humourless comment. After few minutes, she saw him coming back, so she was in a dilemma whether he went to the washroom or he passed by to seek attention as he wanted to show his

tough physique that looked more or less inspired by ARNOLD SCHWARZENEGGER. The girls asked for the bill and were making the payment when the 30-year-old group left.

Haana and Kavya were also leaving when Haana turned back to Kavya near the parking and quoted her that she had been thinking all the way coming out from the cafe-"Look, all the girls are stylishly dressed, we are the only girls who are ordinarily dressed which made us stood out of the crowd either we looked too cute or too shabby; one of the reasons could be why that 30-year-old club stared at us."

Kavya smiled in silence.

They sat in the car and drove back home.

2

Social Media Swagger

A month later, Haana went on a vacation with her family to Bangkok. She felt a new breeze knocking her life. She celebrated her 21st birthday there, in an all-new place for the first time. She was never a romantic person. Even if she was, she did not discover it, but it was then, she began to realise that she was. Whenever she saw love birds, she felt happy that one day she too would find her perfect partner. She always believed in soul mate and knew that somewhere there was a special person made only for her and that her paths would cross with him someday, but she was yet to find out when that was due.

Interestingly, Haana always had a deep faith in the universe, astrology, palmistry, face reading and so on. She was always curious about knowing who and how her soul mate would be. One day she visited one of the temples of Bangkok with her sister Suhaana. When the rest of her family members were outside clicking pictures. She took off her footwear and went inside. The mild fragrance was enormously soothing, Suhaana went upstairs to explore the whole temple when Haana saw the monk meditating, she too sat in front of him and imitated the same posture. She opened her eyes after five minutes when she saw the monk looking at her. She smiled and nodded her head as she had no idea how Buddhist people greeted each other. He too smiled at her and asked her name, she told him. Further, he asked her,

"Do you meditate?"

"No," Haana replied.

"You should, my child, it helps you to explore not only yourself but your potential, your true purpose," the monk suggested.

"Will it help me getting psychic abilities too?" Haana amusingly told to herself.

The monk understood her gesture and smiled, "Child! Every human on planet Earth is different, unique in their way, we all are blessed with some ability or the other, some have talent when some have psychic abilities. Don't focus on either of them. Your intuition is your superpower. Always follow that. Meditation is what helps you discover that, as I have told you. You are blessed with infinite potential; I saw that in you, so I asked. Once you get to know yourself, you will realise how magical you are and miracles are what you will attract."

"And how will I know that?" Haana asked.

He replied with a big smile, took a deep breath and closed his eyes "Meditation."

Haana was unsure whether she should ask a few questions that she had in mind about her life, or not when the monk again opened his eyes and said, "This way you would get answers to all your unanswered questions of life, the situation would unfold naturally and you will get what's best for you."

\#

29 September 2016, 3:45 pm

When back home, Haana developed a habit of meditating three or four times a week. One day she was randomly searching for Sikander on SOCIAL MEDIA. Sikander was

Haana's super senior in college who visited the college the very same day to invite the students to his upcoming concert. As she typed Sikander, a list of the top username of Sikander appeared before her but not the 'Sikander' who she was looking for. There was a display picture in an account that looked appealing to Haana. She clicked on the picture and the profile opened. To her surprise, he was the same guy she had seen in the cafe and joked about, what a sense of humour? She boastfully praised herself. She went through his pictures and was amazed to see how popular he was on social media. Sikander was a social media swagger. After stalking him for a couple of days, she realised, she was being attracted to that guy not because he was muscular, rich or handsome but there was something in him that was beyond what he showed. He was narcissistic for sure but he didn't virtually engage with girls, neither had many female friends. Moreover, his star attitude was his aura. She liked his pickiness.

Days went by, she just thought that he was merely a crush but that attraction didn't fade. He became a book to her that she was interested to read. With much courage, she made a fake account and messaged him, forgetting the fact that why would a popular social media swagger reply to an account with no display picture and friends. Her excitement to know him made her senseless and impatient. Finally, she wrote to him "Hi" but no reply from his end. Later, she made another fake account, that time she tried to be as clever as a fox but he was a lion (actually he was a Leo, which Haana came to know later from his friends). Once again, there was no reply. She approached one of the guys whom she found out to be actively engaging in all of Sikander's pictures with his comments and likes. He told her about his business and also told her that he didn't know much about his personal life, but, yes, he had seen him with a girl a few times. Haana couldn't believe that guy, as it was very hard for her to imagine Sikander with a girl and secondly, the guy himself said that he didn't know about his personal life. Something made Haana believe that Sikander was a heart-broken man who might have loved someone very hard and got ditched. Being a decent guy, he directed his heartbroken energy in a good direction where he focused on his business, bodybuilding, unlike other guys flirting with every other girl and breaking their heart, feeling proud for doing exactly what some other girl had done with them.

Haana knew how accurate she was when long time back she wrote a four liner based on her observation of men where she wrote,

There are two types of men who deal in their way after break-up, the first one are those who break every girl's heart, they get involved in their next relationship and the second are those who redirect their energy in something constructive, they shape their self, their destiny to make sure that they don't encounter the same thing in their life again.

Once again, she approached his other friends, after making sure that they were close to him and inquired about him. Some replied while some did not. Fortunately, they gave her correct information about his profession, family background, birthday and even his address. She got to know enough about him but still, this question was yet to be answered,

"Uske paas Bungalow hai, Gaadi Hai, Bank Balance hai lekin girlfriend hai kya?"

#

One sunny day, Haana went down her home when she saw a car coming. It stopped and a lad appeared. He was Sikander himself. He asked Haana to follow her to the house which was in front of her own house. She silently followed him as he went inside an empty room. She then heard Sikander, saying, **"Tum jo puchna chahte ho uska jawaab Haan hai."** (The answer to your question is yes) and the alarmed clock rang, Haana was dreaming. She didn't know the interpretation of that dream.

However, she wasn't much bothered about it so, that time she did better research, went through his comments, pictures and everything she could find, but nowhere she found any mark of a girl who could be his girlfriend. Well, there were many girls after him for obvious reasons, many of them even posted cheesy comments but they couldn't be suspected.

So, finally, one-day Haana approached one of his cousins Aidh.

Haana thought **'Agar Bade Machli Phasane hai to pehle chote machli phasao.'** (Bait a small fish first if you want a catch a big fish.)

Aidh was in most of Sikander's pictures, they also commented on each other's post and he took a deep interest in replying to Haana. He said he was very close to Sikander and he would ask him to talk to her on one condition.

"What condition?"

"You are going to find a girl for me."

"Okay, Sure."

She asked him about Sikander's relationship status; he confirmed he was single. Again, she asked him, "How can you be so sure?"

He said confidently "If Bhai would have been committed we would have known at home."

Haana felt so pleased with that, Sikander's respect in Haana's eyes increased by ten times. She assumed that Sikander would be a family oriented guy that he would even introduce his girl at home.

While, she was assuming all these, she received a message from Aidh, "Bhai would talk to you now."

3

Late Night Conversation

OCTOBER 2016, 12:30 AM

Haana shared her sister's bedroom as she was too coward to sleep alone in an air condition room at night. She put her mobile on charging next to her sister. She didn't know she would be sleepless that night.

She received a message at thirty-two minutes past twelve.

She woke up when she heard the notification. Sitting beside her half-asleep sister, Haana checked her phone & saw a message "Ji Kahiye! Sabse pata kar rahen hain aap mere bare me."

(Yes, Speak! You are asking everyone about me.)

And that message was from none other, but, Sikander himself. The very Sikander she had been waiting to talk to for so long.

She got so excited that she couldn't control her emotions. The foremost reason was that the message was from Sikander and on top of it, she didn't expect it late at night.

She couldn't utter a single word as everyone was already asleep. She knew she could not make movements; else her sister would wake up.

She immediately took out the phone from the charger and came back inside the quilt.

She paused for a few minutes but failing to control her emotions for long, she texted back to him, "Are you married?"

The big point was not only the unsolved question whether Sikander was in a relationship or not but also that he was married or not? That question was ruling over her mind as she had gone through some of the pictures of Sikander with kids, so she wasn't even sure whether those were his kids or someone else's. That other question wouldn't have risen if that popular Mr Muscle would have been a little smarter and would have captioned his picture. Never-mind, it seemed like he was only concerned about his pictures more than the captions.

The notification bell rang, reply from him, "Yes! I have kids too."

Haana became blank, however, she confirmed, "Then why are you talking to me at this time?"

Sikander was not at least a dull guy, he was smart enough to break the ice, "That's what my wife has asked me to do."

Haana smiled, by that time she was certain that the social media swagger was still a Brahmachari (unmarried.) She stated, "Aap mazak acha kar lete hain."

(You are funny)

Sikander "Aap mere saali hai kya jo aapse mazak karunga?"

(Are you my sister-in-law, that I would joke with you.)

Haana laughed and asked the next question,

"Committed?"

He replied, "Yes!"

Haana made a face and looked at her phone, she didn't know how to react because she wasn't sure whether Sikander was being honest or he was just trying to avoid a conversation from a fangirl (at least in his perception, that was how he would consider her.)

Another message appeared from Sikander on her notification bar, "Why have you been asking about me to my friends?"

She went straightforward and said, "I wanted to know about you."

"Look! I am not as good looking as I look in my pictures."

Haana was more concerned in Sikander's relationship status than other things as everything depended on that.

"If you are committed then why aren't you friends with her on social media?"

"It's because she doesn't use it."

"It means you have a girlfriend. But you said you are a bad looking guy."

Sikander laughed hard and sent laughing emojis to her. He further said, "Haa! Lekin kharab dikhne wale logo ke bhi girlfriend hoti hai."

(Yes! but bad looking guys too have a girlfriend)

Once again, that brought a smile on Haana's face.

Haana gave a thought for a minute, then she remembered what Aidh told her that he wasn't. Also, Aidh replied to her when Sikander was with him, which means Aidh said with his approval. Finally, Haana decided to trust Aidh rather than Sikander.

The percentage of the battery was too low for Haana to carry the conversation forward, she came out of her quilt and once again got her phone on charge. As the phone was next to her sister who was unconscious in her dreams. Haana decided to sit down on the carpet on the floor. It was hardly forty-seconds when she left the quilt but Haana started shivering. She didn't expect a conversation with Sikander in a way that had been happening.

The conversation continued, she admired Sikander's sense of humour.

"Are you serious about your girlfriend?"

Haana was assured by then that Sikander was single, she was just trying to analyse his seriousness and thoughts on love and relationship. "Aur nahi to kya! Warna kabse tumhare sath time pass kar raha hota."

(Of course! Otherwise, I would have been passing my time with you since long)

These lines again helped Sikander in making a soft corner in her heart.

"Is she from the same religion as you?"

"No!"

Hearing that, Haana was on cloud nine, firstly because she knew Sikander was not committed and next supposedly even if he was, he was less likely to get into an inter-religion marriage. (Poor Haana didn't know that our society does accept inter-caste and inter-religion marriages.)

She said "Tab toh Shaadi Nahi ho payegi :D"

Sikander laughed hard and said "Show yourself first, then we will talk"

They both took an equal interest in each other, where Haana went straight forward when Sikander was still being sneaky. Sikander was suspicious about the fact that he was talking to a fake person. She asked Haana what her name was.

For obvious reasons, Haana couldn't disclose her identity to him; not because he would know who she was but because she didn't personally know him. She was unsure that whether the guy she had a crush on was a person worth it or he was just like a bad book with attractive cover but poor content.

She confirmed to Sikander that she was a girl, however, he still wanted to see her.

Haana realised Sikander was not only handsome and witty but also intuitive.

She asked him, "What makes you believe it's a fake account?"

Sikander replied, ":D Your display picture doesn't match your words, so fewer friends."

"Do you judge a girl by her popularity?"

He denied and he still stuck to his first reason i.e. the lack of accord in the picture and the words.

She asked him thrice about his girlfriend as she did not like to be friends with someone who was already involved with someone else.

"On a serious note, if you are genuinely seeing someone, tell me, I won't bother you, your brother Aidh said you are single."

"Yes! I am single, tell me what you want to do?"

Then Sikander proposed for a video call. An electric current hit her from her head to the length of her spine. It was as chilling as the instant headache you can experience if you swallow an ice cube down your throat. That was an unexpected move from Sikander. She denied. She gave an irrelevant excuse on which Sikander joked

"Aren't you wearing your makeup this time?"

She laughed to this but then stopped as it was past three in the morning then and her laughter could wake everyone.

Sikander understood the situation and said, "It's okay if you can't call me right now, I will see you on Sunday at Cannaught Place."

Haana was amazed at what Sikander had uttered. She didn't expect Sikander to come up with something like that. However, she was sure that she couldn't be there on Sunday as she was still in the process of knowing Sikander and meeting him right after a late-night conversation would be unaffordable.

Both of them took equal interest in each other when - *He wanted Answers, She wanted Clarity.*

4

Classroom Drama

Sunday had finally arrived. Haana did not go to see Sikander but she smiled and thought, "Would he be there?" She was unsure that the social media swagger would even remember his meeting with her at Cannaught Place. She overlooked that thought.

The next morning Haana went to the college and narrated her one side crush story to her friend Aaral. Aaral was a fat, chubby girl who always had her nails half-painted, bunked her class, ate all the junk of the world and wondered why she didn't lose even a kilogram but loved her boyfriend Rohit, enough to go against her parents. That was what made Haana share her story with Aaral or could be because they were too lazy to study.

Haana randomly explained about her crush story to Aaral in the class. She told her how she had been stalking him and enquiring about him to his friends, on which Aaral responded, "Itte enquiry mat karo ki tumhare upper he enquiry baith jae."

Aaral insisted to see Sikander's pictures. Haana knew it was safe to show Sikander's pictures to Aaral as she was a loyal girlfriend and wouldn't fall for Sikander (even if she did,

Sikander would not.) However, Haana's mobile battery was already dead. Aaral asked her to not act dumb and that she could tell her Sikander's full name and she would search him up on her phone.

Statistics was a boring class, which seemed even more boring when you have hot topics like SIKANDER to discuss. Haana agreed and asked for Aaral's half-phone (her mobile was too small to be considered as a mobile, it was a black touch screen without keypad so Haana called that a 'half-phone'). As Dr Atwari, a scholar of statistics turned towards the board to write the formula of mean, median and mode. Haana had Aaral's phone hidden below the table. Both her hands were occupied with the phone, one for holding that extra small phone and the second to type that heavy name of SIKANDER. The phone belonged to some 18th century, Haana quoted, "Where did you get this antique piece from?"

"Antique?"

"Of course, is the very first phone Graham Bell invented, it is smaller than the gap between my wrist and palms and the touch doesn't even work anymore."

Aaral crumpled her teeth and gave her an angry look with both her palms closed. When Aaral got angry she looked like a baby which Haana found very cute.

Haana laughed, the professor turned back, raised his brows behind his golden frame. His silence and angry look strongly conveyed, one more noise and you are out. Haana and Aaral are the most disturbing combination of the class. Haana silently went back to her work, she successfully typed Sikander and pressed the "search" button. To Haana's surprise, the only positive thing about Aaral was the fact that her internet speed was as fast as her tongue. Sikander's profile appeared before her. Haana clicked on the display picture and opened his sexiest picture. She pouted and looked at Aaral and pointed towards Mr Muscle's picture from her eyes. Haana put her head down with her hand overlapped to hide from the Professor. Aaral bent towards Haana while she saw the picture and unconsciously utters out loud "wowwwwww."

The whole class stared at Aaral, trying to figure out what did she find so extraordinary in a statistics formula that made her appreciate it so much. Haana realised that Aaral was just a piece of meat without a brain. Aaral knew she had done a mistake and was expecting an unfavourable reaction from the professor. She was waiting for the professor to show her the door and when he did so, she immediately stood up without wasting much time. Dr Atwari did what Aaral wanted. He asked her to leave the class on which Aaral added that it was Haana who had narrated her some story and disturbed her. The professor shifted his focus from Aaral to Haana. Haana's mouth was wide open to an unexpected allegation made on her. He saw the mobile in Haana's hand and reacted as if he saw a murder, raised his voice and shouted at Haana, "Don't you girls know that mobiles are not allowed during the classes?" It was before she could speak and justify herself, the professor nodded in rejection and pointed towards the door and asked them to wait outside. Haana stared at Aaral, closed her notebook and went outside the class.

5

One Day Punishment

The class was over, the professor came out and asked the girls to follow him to the Director's office. Aaral was about to faint when she heard the word "Director" and Haana's mouth was again wide open. She thought **"Itte chote se galati ke itte badi saza?"**

Haana and Aaral neither made any eye contact nor talked to each other while they followed their professor downstairs to the Director's office. All through the way they apologised and assured him not to repeat the same. Dr Atwari without giving any response to the girls, walked down straight, with the attendance register in one hand and his golden frame in the other. He had high standards and so it was against his principle to negotiate with the two most disturbing elements of the class. They reached the director's office, a place that seemed worse than hell. He stepped inside, partially turned back and said, "Rukye Yahe"

(Stop here!)

Aaral's eye caught the nameplate "Director's Room" written in bold, capital and big. She sweat like never before. Haana looked at her properly then and passed an expert comment, "Hope you had sweat like this at the gym, you would have become like me."

Aaral was too depressed to react. All she said was 'if they take my phone, how will I talk to Rohit?'

Haana saw the helplessness on Aaral's face. She knew she was the reason behind all the drama. It was her, who was using Aaral's phone and if her phone would get deposited, how would she show Sikander's pictures to her? :D sorry 'how will she forgive herself?'

The director's room opened like there was a storm inside. Their heartbeat was like never before. Haana never even felt that cold when she received a message from Sikander. Two feet were out, they gradually looked upwards and it was the peon bhaiya who smiled and said- "Chalo Bulawa Aaya Hai."

The two girls looked at each other and went expressionless. Aaral's silence conveyed that Haana was the culprit. Haana was regretting already for what she had done and she never imagined that the matter could come to the Director. They went inside the room with slow steps. The director was on his chair and Dr Atwari in front of him. Haana was a bright and active student, the faculties knew her by her name. The Director looked at her and smiled. She stood straight with her eyes looking at the floor pretending to feel guilty for what she had done. Then to justify themselves on which Aaral went dumb but Haana proceeded – "Sir! Phone uska tha lekin use main kar rahi thi."

Haana lost her mind and behaved weird like she always did when she was stressed. For a minute, she forgot who was she talking to. Suddenly she corrected and framed the same sentence in English, the language which in school days if not spoken, a heavy fine was imposed for the same, "Sir! It was her phone but I was using it."

The director looked astonishingly and asked, "Why were you using her phone?"

Haana was a writer so she knows how to narrate a story.

"Sir! My phone died and I had to inform at home about it, else they would worry if they couldn't get me on call."

Director was still unimpressed. It seemed like he was a sharp story-critic. He asked for the phone. Aaral looked at Haana and took a deep breath as if something was chocking at her chest. Haana protested and also apologised. For a moment Haana became Kareena Kapoor of Jab We Met and thought 'bhai sahab aap convince ho gaye hain ya main aur bolun?'

Finally, the Director showed some pity when he said he had forgiven them but they had to deposit the phone there.

'Still not convinced?'

Haana looked at Aaral. She could see that the embankments of her eyes were full up to the brim and anytime it would flood the regions of her face below her eyes. She requested the Director again. Even then the Director asked them to deposit the phone for a day. Finally, after a 10-minute conversation, Aaral opened her mouth and said in a cracking voice "Sorry Sir" and the very first drop of tear fell from her eyes. Haana realised that the situation had become intense and that Aaral would kill her once they step out of the Director's office, so, apparently, she was in a safe zone. The Director then knew that it was time for some negotiation: "Switch off your phone, write an apology letter and leave. You will get it tomorrow; do not worry about your phone."

Aaral switched off her phone and saw it as if she was seeing her daughter getting married and leaving for "sasuraal." However, she kept it on the Director's big table that reflected the smiling face of Dr Atwari which was a sign of his victory.

6

Unleashing Sikander

NOVEMBER 2016

Pulling aside the window curtains when she woke up in the morning, Haana was pleased by the beautiful weather outside. Haana was a girl who always believed that the weather directly impacted her like most of the people or like everyone else. She inhaled the beautiful fresh air and saw how the clouds were walking across the sky gracefully. Suddenly her eyes caught hold of a beautiful garden with green and fresh grasses everywhere. She saw some of the luxurious cars parked there in colours like red, yellow and green. One of them was a Lamborghini. She took an insight into the whole view where there was a round table and people were sitting there and having breakfast. Then, she saw a muscular man walking around and talking on the phone. She saw him and he looked her back. Interestingly it was Sikander. Haana diverted her eye contact from him but he kept on looking at her for a few seconds. She pulled herself backwards and went inside the dining room all the way thinking how interested Sikander was in her and so he looked at her for a while.

She sat on her dining chair when she saw a stranger talking to her Mom. That guy was some 'Door ka Rishtedaar' of whom Haana came to know after the introduction. The food was arranged for him. When Sikander too appeared, Haana's eyes were wide open to see him. The two men ate the food and were about to leave when Haana's mom asked her 'Door ka Rishtedaar' boy to look for a suitable groom for Haana as they were planning to get her married within a year or two. On which Sikander very friendly spoke to Haana's mom that he too was single.

Haana was very happy to see that and she couldn't hide her smile. A tincture of red spread on her face when she smiled. But soon she was shaken as she opened her eyes and saw her mother standing beside her along with the maid who was cleaning the room.

"Wakeup, what did you see, that you were smiling?" Mom was curious as she asked.

Haana looked here and there and realised how beautiful the dream was. She nodded her head and left the room.

#

Haana's life had a new direction. She was transforming into the best version of herself. Her days started at seeing Sikander's post and ended at thinking about him. She knew Sikander was a strong man, a king who was always in his power. He was a lion who sat in silence and she was ready to tame him. She knew he was worth taking the challenge, her eyes were on the price. She knew men like Sikander doesn't exist anymore. He had all that a girl would ask for. However, she did not want to have him easily. She wanted him to pursue and approach her the way she did. She knew she was not one of those girls who like Sikander for all his wealth, physique, popularity but for the man he was. She never wanted to date him or be with him for any selfish reason, rather, she wanted to marry him ever since she realised that she was fond of him. She wanted to have a long-lasting bond with him. She did not want to be one of his girls but his only girl. Therefore, she knew Sikander was a trophy that she would only get when she would win the competition of her life.

Haana was always an ambitious girl, but she became even more ambitious. She wanted to be financially stable in her life, irrespective of the fact that she belonged to a well-off family where she had all the luxuries, yet she wanted to stand on her own feet. It was before she belonged to anyone whom she would marry, she wanted to be known as Haana, rather than Mrs X or Y. She didn't want the tag of her future husband's name.

She wanted to be a government servant which would fetch her power, money and a position in the society so that she could stand with Sikander and have a life of her own. She did not want to be one of those girls who had to be dependent on their parents first and then on their husbands post-marriage. She wanted to be so strong that she could not only help herself but the needy too.

She came to know about Sikander's birthday which was on 3rd August and there was still a few months. By that time, Haana would have so many things to do. She had to qualify the UPSC examination so that she could get a decent position by that time and she would be earning so that when she would meet Sikander on his birthday she could gift him an expensive watch as she knew Sikander loved expensive shit.

Her college exams were scheduled to happen in December. She decided to join the coaching from January onwards - new year, so energy to do something great.

Sikander was revolving around her mind like a satellite around a planet. She was unable to name that situation-was it love or crush or coincidence or attraction, but finally, she figured it out - *'It's the love that attracts, Not the attraction that loves.'*

Then, she was to decide between love and crush, as coincidence was not what she believed in. She knew everything that ever happened to a human, had a purpose to serve in their life. Every minor omen led towards a big revolution. So, a 6 feet tall omen couldn't just be a coincidence, he surely had a purpose in her life, bigger than his biceps. Haana had a strong belief about Sikander that he had not always been the man he chose to show the world or how he then was. The light behind his stardom was a result of some dark struggle. Haana had a strong intuition that the heartthrob surely might have been heartbroken at least once in his life. What made her feel strong was when he said about not trusting people in their late-night conversation that day-

(The late-night conversation)

"Are you serious towards your girlfriend?"

"Of course! Warna kabse tumhare sath time pass kar raha hota."

"Will you marry her?"

"If possible, yes. Otherwise, I will marry someone else."

"But you said you are serious for her?"

"Yes! But what if she leaves me?"

"Why will she leave you? You have everything a girl can ever ask for."

":P you never know, you cannot trust anyone these days, anything can happen."

"*You cannot trust anyone these days, anything can happen.*" - That line left a deep impact on Haana's mind and made her double think before she concluded that her perception towards Sikander was almost accurate.

(Continues)

"I will see you at CP and then decide whether we can be friends or not," Sikander proposed.

"Why Sunday? Anything special?"

"I don't get time on weekdays, so Sunday."

"Ah! I see. What are you busy with?"

"I get up late, go to the gym, come back in the evening and go to Cafe Bronze."

Haana got her point 'Cafe Bronze' - the place where she saw him for the first time.

She asked, "Do you go there every day?"

"Yes! Almost"

"With girls?"

"Sometimes"

Haana questioned with a sense of possessiveness, "And who are those girls?"

"I hire them on rent," Sikander replied. Haana laughed silently.

"Of course those are friends; or who else they can be?"

Haana was happy with the answer.

"Are you coming for the video call or not?"

"Look, my sister is here, I can't."

"Kindly don't make excuses. Ok! Send me your picture."

After Haana sent her a couple of cute pictures of some other girl, she asked: "Now we can be friends, right?"

"No."

"But I look so cute."

"Aap Mujhe lalaach de rahe ho ke aap cute ho?"

(Are you bribing me that you are cute?)

"Send me your picture."

Haana knew Sikander was a challenging game, it wasn't easy to fool him and she was anyways loving that challenge.

"What if I send you another picture and claim it to be mine, how will you differentiate?"

"You raise both your hands on your head just like this emoji (he set an emoji) and then click, I will know it's you, simple."

26

Sikander clarified, "I don't talk to fake people, I don't even know whether you are a boy or a girl."

Haana thought about the new twist "boy?" and wondered why will a boy be interested in Sikander. In the first place, it was difficult to gain his trust in her being an actual girl or fake girl on top of it that, a new twist "boy."

She asked for a clarification "Boy? Why will I be a boy? And why would a boy message you."

"I don't know, but this has happened to me before some boys have messaged me, they fell for my physique."

Haana went crazy over that statement of Sikander and laughed so hard that her eyes got filled with water. She told Sikander how funny it was.

7

Blocked

Haana knew Sikander's reaction was valid. How could he talk to a person he didn't know. On top of it, she did not go to see him at CP on Sunday. To take a leap of faith, she messaged him again.

Sikander asked her the most unexpected question
"Why didn't you come on Sunday?"

Haana was surprised to see this message, she did not know the man she thought wouldn't even remember about the day asked for the reason behind her absence, it meant he was there on Sunday and waited for her.

Haana was touched and typed,

"Look! I understand you are right, it's daunting to talk to someone whom you don't even know but kindly think from my perspective, how can I visit you only after a late-night conversation?"

That time Sikander was annoyed,

"Don't act like a child, you are a grown-up."

Haana was pleased to see that concerning behaviour of Sikander which meant he was there to see her, and he too was interested in knowing her but...

Another notification, Sikander's message: "I cannot carry forward the conversation with someone I don't even know, please don't mind but I am blocking you."

#

Haana was reflecting upon the situation, she thought what a wonderful and kind human Sikander was, even if he had to block Haana, how politely Sikander did that too.

"Don't mind but I am blocking you."

"Please don't mind but I am blocking you."

.....wow! what a man

Haana was confirmed that her curiosity of reading the book called Sikander was fruitful. He was not just an attractive cover but also a wonderful content. She decided not to trouble him again. One day when randomly going through his old pictures, she saw one of his pictures where the caption had a grammatical error. Haana couldn't resist but messaged Sikander from another fake account, asking him to correct his mistake. Sikander replied thankfully and said, "Thank You, Bro!"

Haana was confused and said, "BRO? I am a girl, not bro."

Sikander replied with a laughing emoji, ":D I know."

"How?"

"You are the same girl I had blocked a few days back."

Haana was stunned with Sikander's intuition and asked him, "Then why did you reply?"

"It was you who wanted to talk not me, you have been messaging me. If you don't have the guts then why do you message me?"

Haana was moved by that statement and responded, "I did not expect this from you."

"You don't have to expect anything from me."Haana couldn't believe that it was the same Sikander she was fond of; she was unaware of that aspect of Sikander or was she unaware that Sikander had that furious aspect too?

The only thing Haana thought of Sikander at that point of time was, 'Don't get carried away with the Light of your Stardom, It can lead you towards Darkness.'

8

Taking A Leap of Faith

DECEMBER 2016

Haana was done with Sikander but deep inside her heart, she had the feeling of "what if?" She was a kind of person who might commit the mistake and say "Oops!" rather than not trying what she wanted and living with a "what if?" for the rest of her life. She knew Sikander was upset, however, she too was helpless. She would have disclosed her identity if things could have been smoother. She did not want to regret all her life for not telling Sikander who she was. She decided to approach Sikander by herself as Haana. Meanwhile, she was planning how to do all that, she went to Aidh's account and liked his pictures with Sikander. To return her favour, Aidh liked dozens of Haana's pictures and followed her. With much surprise, she received a message from Aidh,
"Hello!"
Haana did not know how to react as she was never interested in Aidh but Sikander. However, she messaged Aaral and informed about Aidh's message. Acting a so-called "crush guru" if not love-guru, Aaral adviced Haana to talk to Aidh ignorantly. Haana asked her to explain how

ignorant she should be. Aaral explained not to be sweet yet reply to his messages to give a feeling that she was just being friendly.

Haana did not like her idea. She believed rather than making him feel small by doing something like that, it would be better not to respond, therefore, she ignored both Aaral's stupid advice and Aidh's message.

Her vision became clear. She finally gathered much courage to approach Sikander as herself and was prepared that even if Sikander wouldn't reply to her, at least she wouldn't regret not trying. The year was at the end and that she could start the new year with no Sikander in it. She would dump Sikander as a bad habit.

She typed and edited the message to and fro. Her heart was beating faster and her hands were shivering, but finally, she typed and sent

"You were there in Cafe Bronze?"

After half an hour, she received a message from Sikander. Seeing Sikander's name on her real account in her phone gave her butterflies, she first took the screenshot and then opened the message, which read "When?"

Without wasting much time, she replied: "I don't know."

"Hmm"

Haana thought 'did he see me that day so he knows when I am talking about?' She went straightforward and threw a millennium question to Sikander, unconsciously in the exact pattern as she asked from a fake account.

"Are you taken?"

Sikander went blank and asked "What?"

She went easy that time and asked, "Married?"

"No."

That was what she was expecting from him and also on her next question.

"Committed?"

"Yes!"

Haana did not feel anything on that answer, neither disguise nor loss, no pain and for sure no gain. She still was unsure about the authenticity of that answer. She was in a dilemma whether Sikander was seeing someone else or he was just trying to avoid another conversation from a girl.

"Fine someone was interested."

"Who?"

"You don't know her."

However, the only unexpected element was Sikander's curiosity burning in him, which he failed to hide and asked again, "But tell me who is she?"

Haana was not happy because there was no point in carrying forward the conversation with someone who already belonged to someone else, still, she had the last words, "Makes no difference, you already have someone else."

One thing that struck Haana was the fact that she dreamt of it. She dreamt of an empty room where Sikander himself took her name and said that the answer to her question is yes. That was what exactly he told her when she asked him about his relationship status. Did that mean that she already got the answer from the universe on the most bothering question of her life? How could she avoid such an omen? Hadn't she approached Sikander in person, how would Sikander know there was a girl called Haana who was so fond of him. *So, did it happen for the Better or the Worse?*

9

Insecure from a Fictitious Character

21 DECEMBER 2016

It was Suhaana's birthday. Haana wished her on WhatsApp as Suhaana had already left for office. Haana kept her phone on the dining table when she received a message around four in the evening. She was expecting a 'Thank You' message from Suhaana but it was not the birthday girl rather it was a message from Aidh.

"Hello!"

The very same message, however, that time Haana was in dilemma whether it was actually from Aidh or it was Sikander who asked Aidh to send on his behalf as Haana knew Sikander was too proud if not shy, to make the first move.

Haana replied in the most uninteresting tone, "Do I know you?"

"No!" Aidh confirmed. Further, he added, "My brother was asking about you."

"Which brother?" Haana asked in a relaxed tone though she knew who the brother was.

"Sikander."

"Is he your brother?"

Haana pretended to ask their relation, though Aidh was the first person Haana knew was the closest to Sikander.

"What was he asking?" Haana asked again with butterflies in her stomach.

"Yes! he is my brother. He was asking that may I know you."

Haana couldn't resist acting as an English teacher and once again corrected him out of her habit, "You mean to say that do you know me?"

That time Aidh didn't want to sound like a fool, so he played safe and quite smartly answered her in two letters, "Hm." He added, "I told him that I don't know you."

To sound uninterested, Haana replied "Ok!"

Aidh continued, "Yup, but you are sweet."

(Ab ye to zyada hogaya, Haana thought)

To cease any uncertain chance if at all Aidh was willing to take, Haana replied, "Excuse Me?"

This made Aidh disappointed and sad maybe. But to make Aidh vomit about all that Sikander asked him about her, she continued the conversation, "Why did he ask you whether you know me or not?"

"I liked your pictures and you have been messaging him, that's why."

Oh Shucks! Ab to raita phail gaya

Haana thought it was only between Sikander and her, but now Aidh was also involved. That guy had been playing a major supporting character in their crush story right from the beginning.

Haana's tone drastically changed, from acting as hard to get to a softer version. Haana was a writer, so it was not difficult to narrate a story, she wouldn't get a chance better than that to showcase her talent spontaneously, therefore she continued, "Actuallyyyyy naa, I texted him on behalf of my friend."

She continued, "A friend of mine is interested in Sikander. She is committed but she was casually taking a chance, so she didn't do by herself rather asked me to."

She wasn't expecting that from the other side but a bomb was thrown at her by Aidh,

"Who is your friend?"

Ignoring his question, Haana stated, "But Sikander clarified that he is committed."

Without even wasting a minute, Aidh replied within exactly 30 seconds, "Who told you he is committed?"

(Haana ke mann me ek laddo phoota)

"He is single right now."

(Doosra laddoo bhi phoota)

So to have transparency over the situation, Haana said, "Sikander himself confessed that, you can ask him, though I did not like asking him directly about his relationship status."

What made Haana came up with such lame excuses? Who in the world makes such dumb excuses?

Aidh acting as a massakali between Sikander and Haana, "He must be kidding."

Something went too wrong with Haana and she continued with her fake and lame excuse. It was out of the happiness and excitement to hear that Sikander was single, Haana lost control over her emotions.

"She was a friend, so I had to do that else I wouldn't have, she just went too bananas over him."

Aidh courteously, "Ok."

Next, he happened to become an interviewer and asked, "Tell me something about yourself."

In the most uninteresting tone and to convey her unbothered nature towards Aidh, she wrote a single letter which would be enough for Aidh to understand how uninterested she was towards Aidh, "Y?"

Either he was dumb or was too interested in Haana, he did not get her mental message and replied, "Because I wanted to know you."

That time Haana went straightforward and asked, "Don't mind but why should I tell you, why do you want to know me?"

Aidh was no less than DDLJ ka Shah Rukh Khan, he came with such cheesy and flattering lines, "Friendship karne se pehle friend ke bare me janna zaroori hota hai." (It's important to know about your friend before making friends with them.)

Haana heard those lines and thought, 'If Late Yash Chopra would have been alive, he would surely have cast him as a writer in one of his upcoming movies.'

To show her interest in Sikander over Aidh, she questioned, "Who wants to be friends with me, you or Sikander?"

"Whatever you feel like, he is my brother."

"You initiated for friendship, how would I know whether you are asking for yourself or your brother?"

"No! I am asking for myself."

"Don't mind but I am not interested."

Aidh was a not a dumb guy, after all, he was Sikander's brother, he proved it when he replied, "No problem if you don't want to be friends with me. It was your friend who was approaching for Bhai."

Haana went furious over a girl who doesn't even exist. For the first time she was feeling insecure from a fictitious character that she made by herself, every time there happened to be chance about her and Sikander. 'Why was your friend bumping in between?'

"She is not a friend, just an acquaintance she wanted to pass her time in Delhi."

Aidh was a sweet person or at least that's what he was showing when he told Haana, "Thank God, you clarified all these things right now I don't like to break friendship later."

Once again, Haana typed the two uninterested letters, "hm."

"I am not interested in your friend."

Haana was impressed with this attitude.

"Ok! I know. Who sends a message for an unknown?"

The only thing that Haana felt was "Kaash yeh dharti khul jae aur main isme dhas jau."

Aidh was not a dumbo. He made out it was Haana.

Haana again confronted the very same thing, "She was neither an unknown nor a friend."

"Ok!"

"Anything else?"

"Nothing."

"Take Care Bye!"

#

Things went back to from where it all started. Sikander confessed he was seeing someone when Aidh surely said he wasn't. The same dilemma, but different time. The last hope Haana had to know about Sikander's relationship status was from Sikander himself but things have become even more complicated by then.

10

Surprises for Sikander

8 JANUARY 2017

Haana joined the UPSC coaching. She knew Sikander was interested in no girl including her and as far as his relationship status was concerned, she still didn't know the answer. As planned, she has to join the coaching to qualify the exam and take her life to the next level as she still had faith that if destiny had written them to be together, they would meet. But Haana was not hopeful though yet she had it somewhere in her mind 'if they meet on Sikander's birthday' when she had already planned a secret party and a wristwatch to gift him. Now, her focus was not on Sikander but herself, her career. Sikander was a fitness freak, Haana was already blessed with a fit body, however, she too hit the gym, sweat for hours to get a perfect shape that she deserves to be in. She did not want to take any chance with her and Sikander's relation. He was influencing her in her day to day life, whatever Haana found good about Sikander, she learnt it from him and adapted it in her daily life. That way Sikander turned from her crush to her days.

Physically, she never made a move towards Sikander but mentally she was still hoping for clarity. Her question was still unanswered. Sikander already told her that he was taken, even if he wasn't, it meant he was not interested in Haana which further made no sense on Haana's part to approach him. Even after knowing all those things, Haana was unable to move into a different direction, rather she was gravitating towards Sikander even more. All she knew was that it was a pure fondness.

Haana did not know what to do about the situation, why was she unable to forget a mere crush, what purpose Sikander had in her life. *She knew, she was searching for her answers in unanswered questions of life.*

Nevertheless, Haana was a believer, she had a deep faith in the universe. She always prayed to the universe before making any big or small decisions. Whenever she got stuck in dilemma, she asked the universe - 'If it's not good for me, kindly remove all the attachment I have towards it but if it is meant for me, keep me patient, Amen.'

Sikander was one of the major decisions and other things that happened to Haana. Therefore she became particular and asked the universe to give her clarity and continued, 'If Sikander is not meant for me, kindly remove all the attachment I have towards him, detach my chords from him, but if he is meant for me, keep me patient and make me waiting, give me signs, show me the truth, Amen.'

Haana kept on asking and praying when one day when she was again stalking Sikander on his social media profile. She opened one of his friend's profile randomly and saw a comment, she opened the profile of the user who commented and was shocked to see the girl with Sikander next to her. She immediately scrolled down the profile and saw dozens of pictures wherein every picture it's either the girl crossing her hands over Sikander's neck or it's Sikander resting over her shoulder. The postures were powerful enough to convey their relationship. For the first time, Haana's eyes were filled with tears because of Sikander. She continued to see the details in the profile when she realised that her unanswered question got answered and the girl's profile mentioned their three years of relationship. The first drop of tear fell from her eyes. Her heart denied continuing reading and seeing the pictures when her mind asked her to continue. That time she followed her mind and went on. After researching for a few more minutes, she realised that the girl had already been introduced to Sikander's family which was a major indication about the seriousness of their relationship. Haana was guided by the universe. She immediately went inside her bedroom, locked herself and called Aaral, explained the whole situation of what she saw and read. Aaral patiently listened to her and understood that Haana wanted more of a listener at that point of time rather than a consultant. She wanted to be heard. Aaral listened and consoled her.

Haana was a practical girl. She always followed her heart but always considered her mind though. She knew it was stupid of her to cry over that when Sikander had already confessed about his relationship status to her. He gave her no false hope. It was her overthinking that was making her cry. It was her built imagination, fantasies and dreams that broke into pieces. She said all those things to Aaral too.

#

Everything changed overnight. Social media was not a social place for Haana anymore, rather she isolated herself. What seemed and felt like ambition yesterday, then felt like baggage. However, she did not give up. She continued, she denied compromising her dreams for a minor heartache. She had a belief that '*Dreams cannot be broken, because of broken dreams.*'

She proceeded with her life like before but with a different vision. Haana tends to be matured with the damage and said to herself, '*He might not be the Man in my DESTINY but he is the Man of my DREAMS.*'

11

Surprise turned Shock

Haana's zeal to qualify the exams was higher than before. She was the challenge that she wished for rather than Sikander, unlike before. The month next was her exams. She took no risk, whether it was a rainy or a sunny day, whether she was fit or ill, she never took a leave from her coaching, she went to her classes, no matter what. She might have missed her college at times, but she wouldn't miss her coaching, not even in her worst nightmare.

One morning Haana woke up and wrote down in a writing app in her phone about the last night dream where she had seen a feast out of Cafe Bronze. She saw her mother sitting in a nearby restaurant when she went to order something and Sikander appeared to her mother, talked to her about something and when her mother asked about his marital status, he replied he was single and if she had any girl in mind, he would like to see that girl.

After writing, Haana related it, how it could be connected to Sikander's interest in her. She scrolled up the page and read how a couple of months back she had noted down a few of the other dreams about Sikander and in one of them Haana was at Cafe Bronze and how coincidentally she had seen Sikander in White Shirt & Blue Denim sitting on a table alone. Then in another one where Haana attended a wedding ceremony of some friend after which Sikander's mother asked Haana's mother to find a good girl for Sikander to get married with (looking at Haana.) On which Haana said to his mother that Sikander was already involved with someone else. Sikander looked at Haana's mother and told her that he was with someone else but he would marry a girl whom his mom wanted him to marry.

April 2017

Finally, it was the day of the exam. She knew deep inside that she wanted to be independent but that was not how it was supposed to be. She went to the examination centre, took the examination but did not attempt the questions, not even those whose answers she had known. She got to realise, that was not what she wanted to do. It could not fetch her true contentment and satisfaction. All that time she was busy thinking about her future, what she wanted to do and how would she discover her purpose.

#

August 2017

Haana's family was invited for dinner at Cafe Bronze, the same place, but a year back where everything started. However, as she had already shattered Sikander from her life if not her heart, she didn't feel nostalgic anymore. It was when she was busy clicking pictures with the host, she saw a girl sitting at the extreme right corner with a cup of coffee on the table who looked exactly like the girl who was with Sikander in the pictures.

Meanwhile, Haana was figuring out whether she was the same girl or not when she saw a muscular guy pulled the chair and sat before her and it was Sikander, whose back was visible to Haana. However, Sikander couldn't notice her. Haana knew Sikander was nothing but an illusion for her. She already had left his thoughts from her mind and she quoted *'Only when she saw him over a Cup of Coffee with someone else, she realised Love was not her Cup of Tea.'*

Haana went back home and gave a thought on what people said was correct **The more you run from something, the more it follows you.'**

When she had finally given up on Sikander, when she no more took interest in him, when she was underway finding the purpose and meaning of her life, Sikander bumped into her life again, that time with his girlfriend. At least, that was not okay, seeing him once again in her life was bearable but the sight with his girlfriend was intolerable. She dropped those thoughts from her mind and began looking at the pictures she clicked at the dinner. It was when she was flipping her gallery, suddenly her eyes caught the same date 3rd August 2017.

That was not happening.... no...no...

She took a pillow, kept it on her face and shouted. She was a volcano who was supposed to erupt for her own highest good and she did that, and, why wouldn't she?

It was third August, Sikander's birthday and she was at the same place where they met for the first time, where everything originated. She made so many plans for Sikander's birthday. Her journey of the last few months appeared before her. Her willingness to qualify the UPSC examination so that she could attain a good position, power, and money in society. Her fantasy of gifting Sikander expensive gifts; nothing existed anymore. Ironically, Sikander too was there the same day but with his girlfriend.

What game was the universe playing with Haana?

12

College Scenes

Haana's new college re-opened. She proceeded with M.Com for her masters after completion of her B.Com. She made new friends, a new college, a new kick in her life - everything was new. 14th August, Haana's college participated in the intercultural program at another college, where different colleges in the city participated in different events. This intercultural program is held for three consecutive days every year. It was her very first time, although she did not participate in any of the events, some of her friends did, so, she went to cheer for them and the college. Getting ready for the competition early in the morning, catching up with friends in the college and then leaving for the competition together, was undoubtedly a feeling of unity. They drove to four kilometres to the event. At the entrance, there were local students of the college who were wearing the college sport's t-shirt and sitting on the other side of the table distributing passes and tokens for the participants. The volunteers stood at every corner of the campus and their uniform differentiated them from the students of the guest college. They were ready to help anyone looking for guidance regarding the programs. Haana along with her group of friends went inside, collected their passes (not token as she was not a participant.) They moved inside and saw the beautiful campus. They still had to wait half an hour for the program to start so they bought tea and headed towards the big green ground where they encountered students doing the last practice for the sports. She looked at the ground when her eyes caught a girl whose hands were in two shades, the brown and the dark brown. Haana minutely noticed her hand from far for some time and tapped on Goher's shoulders, her new college friend, to show her the same. Goher looked at the direction and made a guess, "It could be sun tan. The girl must be practicing for quite a long time here at the ground and she might have got tanned."

#

Haana along with her group of friends were sitting and cheering for their friends who were contestants in the sports. Haana clicked a few pictures, sorted out the best one and posted it on her social media handle. After 10 minutes, something hit her intuitively and she from within was propelled to visit Sikander's profile after a long time, and out of surprise, she noticed that 2 minutes right after she posted her picture, Sikander too made a post. On a span of 2 minutes? A coincidence? Maybe Haana thought.

The pain was relieved to a major extent. Haana no more felt a sense of anxiety in visiting Sikander's profile to see his updates and pictures.

Seemed like time had healed her.

13

Lion Chasing the Girl

Haana threw a party on her birthday. When she was back home, she posted those enjoying moments with her new friends. Two days later she saw Sikander posting pictures with his friend. Interestingly the colour of his dress was same to what Haana wore on her birthday together with the caption being almost similar. An alert bell rang in Haana's mind. Co-incidence once again? That too so strong, no ways, something was cooking at the other side of the screen.

Was their story restarting?

That time the lion was chasing the girl.

However, it could be a coincidence, maybe just two incidents recently and how could she suspect it?

But it didn't end there, she continued to notice the pattern. It became so often that whenever Haana posted anything, Sikander's next post was similar to it. Haana had no clue what exactly was happening. Had Sikander made a comeback? That came so intensifying that one-day Haana posted a picture in blue denim and red sweatshirt at Cafe Bronze, the place where they met for the first time. The next evening when she opened Sikander's profile, she saw his picture at the very same place in the colours i.e. blue denim and a red T-shirt. My God! Was he giving me mixed signals? Did he find out that I liked him? Did he like me back?

All those thoughts were already in Haana's mind, when one evening Haana went to the newly opened cafe, a double storey cafe with Suhaana and friends and they all settled at the ground floor. Live music was going on, Haana was cheering for the singers in full mood with Suhaana. They clicked photographs, enjoyed and came back home.

The next day when Haana visited Sikander's profile, she saw him posted a picture of him about the last night at the same place at around 9 pm.

'Omg! Does it mean he too was there when I was in? I was at the ground floor when he was upstairs. Did he know I was there? Did he come intentionally or it was a coincidence.' The confusion increased, earlier it was whether Sikander was doing all that but then whether it was Sikander or the Universe itself.

All those thoughts were revolving around Haana's mind.

Sikander never initiated. Haana never returned but their
Social Media Game of Love continued.

#

December 2017

Things had changed, the story had twisted, characters had changed their role, it was more than a year. Suhaana turned 26 that day, she threw a small party for Haana and friends. Haana was at the venue enjoying with everyone when she noticed a couple in the corner talking to a lady, who seemed to look very interested in the couple. Haana stared there for around five minutes and was unable to understand what deep conversation they were having. Finally, the couple left, Haana asked her friends to excuse her. She went to the lady and as she reached her, she saw there were cards and stones on the table and she was no ordinary lady. She asked her curiously, "Are you an astrologer?"

The lady smiled and responded, "No! I am a tarot card reader"

"Oops! Haana bit her lower lips and apologised.

"No problem," the lady smiled and asked her to sit.

Haana sat down and asked her "How does it work?"

"50 Bucks for 1 question."

The lady came straight away to business, what a business-minded lady, Haana thought.

"Think of a question in your mind, then pick a card"

"Sounds exciting."

Haana was checking the authenticity of the card reader, she already knew the answer to her first question, yet she thought "Is Sikander interested in me?" She sighed at the lady and showed a thumb up. The lady leaned over her chair and asked her to pick three cards. She was confused, she saw the whole deck of cards arranged in a semi-circle manner. She thought for some time and then she finally picked three cards and gave it to the reader. The lady flipped the cards and looked at Haana and showed a thumb up,

"The answer to your question is YES."

Haana was happy yet acted normal as it did not surprise her, because she already knew the answer.

Nevertheless, she was excited about the second question, she showed her interest to the reader who was shuffling the cards. Once she was done, she asked Haana for the second question.

She explained that she liked a guy, and she wanted to know whether he was stalking her on social media or not.

The reader asked for the boy's name, however, she denied. The lady insisted and told her if she could know his name, she would get more clarity over the situation and she could deliver a clear message. "He is no-one to me. I suspect he likes me from the mixed signals he has been giving to me yet I am unsure, it could be my overthinking as well. He already belongs to someone else; I don't have any right over him. It would be unethical if I mention someone's name who is none to me. Had he been my friend, I would have told you his name but in this case, I don't find it appropriate to take his name."

The tarot card reader raised her brow and made a gesture from her mouth as if she got her point and she appreciated it. Further, the reader closed her eyes, read something that Haana made out from muttering lips of the reader. That time the reader herself pulled out three cards, flipped it and kept it before her.

She was feeling anxious, cold and excited at the same time. Her eyes were wide open and she couldn't wait for the reader to speak up. The reader took a deep breath, smiled and said "Interesting cards."

"Yes! he is stalking you and he likes you a lottttt…"

Her emphasis on 'a lot' made Haana feel on cloud nine.

"Why isn't he making any move then? He's also committed."

The reader took off her glasses and explained to her, "This could be the reason why he isn't making any move. But he is interested in you. It might be his commitment towards his girl that is restricting himself from coming towards you. The girl might do things for him and love him, which could be the reason why he doesn't want to break her heart. He is stalking you. He knows where you are and what you are up to in your life currently. Also, if ever they break up, it's you who have to make the first move."

That was what Haana didn't want to hear. She already made a move and she was not ready for another chance. If he would be interested, he would come. She had already showed him her interest before. Being a man if he couldn't come, it meant he was unsure and she didn't want to be with a man who was unsure of her or who was too shy/ proud to make the first move. She wanted to be her man's only girl not one of his girls.

Haana had a philosophy- 'Always Fight for your LOVE, never COMPETE for it'

#

The tarot card session just ended when Haana's phone rang and she went towards the washroom to receive it. She was on call when she saw a tall man walking inside the venue, her eyes froze on him. He was none other but Sikander. He did not see her as she was standing in the corner. Haana also noticed a girl with him. She was not his girlfriend; Haana was sure about it. The message delivered by the tarot reader just showed up in real. Haana's faith became stronger that *'Her mind was playing games with her, but, deep inside her, her heart knew that he searched for her every time she tried to hide.'*

The question she asked about him, became a reality when he came and gave the answer. She never thought she would inquire about him and he would come all the way to show himself to her.

It was her! It was her! She could feel how everything was turning out to be so real. She was the girl whom Haana had seen in her dream. Her fading memories were becoming fresh and she could visualise everything right from the time she was in the market to the time she had seen Sikander stalking her after he had just passed by her. 'Omg! Such Psychic abilities I have? Haana asked herself or the universe guiding me all through?'

Then, Haana recalled the same day from the last year when she was crying, she gave up all the hopes and then it was Sikander who was stalking her. Why?

14

An Interaction with Mr Show-off

A cricket match was held at the stadium. Haana along with Kaavya went there. Personally, Haana had no serious interest in cricket but it's Kavya who took a lot of interest in Mr Sharma (Virat Kohli.) The match began, Haana was waiting for it to get over. Kaavya had her eyes on Virat Kohli. Haana was getting bored. A younger guy came and sat beside her. He wore a formal dark blue trouser and a full sleeve light blue shirt, hair properly combed using a hair gel and he was showing his iPhone X like every other iPhone users.

"When will the match get over, so that I can go and visit the players personally, he murmured.

Haana turned and gave him an indifferent look. Haana was a sandwich between Mr Show-off and Kavya. She glanced at him and then looked back at the game.

"Oh God!" when will it end, he told to himself, as if he was tensed and excited at the same time.

Haana couldn't control and asked, "Why did you come then?"

"My friend dragged me here. I had plans to directly visit the players at their hotel."

Haana nodded her head.

"I have no fondness towards them."

Haana gave him a weird look and asked, "Then why do you wanna meet them?"

"Because I want to click pictures with them, selfies."

"Hain?" Haana gestured.

"You aren't fond of them, yet you want to take selfies with them, strange."

"Only for show off."

Haana pouted, her eyes became small, she again looked at him and waited for him to answer.

"Yes! I have so many pictures with Indian celebrities, I post them on my social media handles. I will click selfies with these players too and I will post."

"Ohkayyyyy! And how will it help you?"

"It would show people how powerful my contacts are, would fetch me respect. You won't believe I already have taken pictures with so many celebs."

He opened his iPhone X and showed Haana his facebook pictures with a famous Indian heroine to make her believe about his statement.

Haana saw it and said, "hm."

He kept on boasting about how he met that Indian celeb, gave her a bouquet and that she knew him by his name.

"What is your name?" Haana asked.

"Arjun. Your name Ma'am?" he asked.

Haana gave it a pause trying to figure out whether she should tell her name or not but then she told him.

"Nice name, different haan," he replied and added, "You know I like to maintain contact with these rich people and personally know many of them."

Once again Haana just nodded her head as she was clueless why that guy had been boasting before her from the last 10 minutes.

"One of my friends own a Ferrari".

"Oh!"

"Yes, he is a musician."

"Okay! I did not know we have Ferrari, here in Delhi too. All I know that the most expensive car we have is Lamborghini."

"Yes! Owned by that Sikander."

Haana was alert, "What! You know him?"

"YES."

"How do you know he has a Lamborghini?" he cross-questioned Haana.

Haana probably was already prepared with the answer, "Actually, I know he is some social media swagger, saw it on his posts."

"Acha!"

"By the way, do you know him personally?" Haana asked.

"Not really but I have met him several times either at parties or at events. He is a nice guy, but he is very powerful, involved in politics too."

Haana asked him to excuse her as she had to attend a call. The guy too moved. Meanwhile, Kaavya was busy watching the match.

'Once again Sikander?' Haana whispered as if it was her soliloquy.

15

The Longing Proposal

The next day she went to her college and was selected as one of the five most talented people in the college because she was an amazing writer. Her faculty recommended her name to the lady who was a renowned entrepreneur and sponsored the competition. Haana went inside the library along with four other students where the lady waited for a one to one interaction. They introduced themselves to the lady and vice versa.

A multiple-choice questionnaire was distributed to all of them which had basic questions to judge their personality.

The students hardly took 5-7 minutes to answer and submit the questionnaire. The lady told the students that whoever reached the cut off score, would get a call from her.

#

Haana had different specialisation than her friends. She did not have a class when her friends were attending theirs. She went to the college ground and sat on the stairs. She looked at the undergraduate students practicing there. At times, she also cheered the basket-ball players she knew. She saw two girls playing cards on the stairs below her, she remembered what the tarot card reader told her about

Sikander, then Haana remembered how she fantasised Sikander proposing her.

Stood at the very same cafe with flowers all over the wall, dim lights, fragranced candles lit all over, Haana in her beautiful gown unable to make out why Sikander had called her there. A car stopped by, a pair of shiny black formal shoes stepped out. It was Sikander in a black tuxedo with his glasses on, clean shaved, looking 100X times handsome than he was. He came close to Haana with confidence, took off his glasses, looked directly in her eyes and bent down on his knees, opened a box with a ring to propose her. That was when the petals of the flowers fell on her, lights turned on and she saw Sikander with a smile on her face and tears in her eyes. Sikander lifted her and they probably lived happily ever after.

"Hello, Writer Sahiba."

Haana heard a voice and looked at her right. Haana looked at found it was Kunal, the rich guy who rarely comes to the college and whenever he did, he left early, providing excuses like he either had to attend a meeting or meet a client.

"Hello Kunal!"

"Why are you sitting here?"

"My lecture is over."

"Alright, did you go to see the match?"

"Yes!"

"Enjoyed?"

"Not really. I don't even know ABCD of cricket, I reacted as per the audience, whenever my friend shouted in excitement, I too cheered for them when she was quiet so was I."

"By the way, do you know a boy name Arjun?"

"Which Arjun?" Kunal's eyes became small as if he was trying to recall something.

"I don't personally know him, he told me he has a friend who owns a Ferrari, so I thought you might know him."

"AHH! Did he mention my name or anything else?

"Not your name, but yes, he mentioned that he is friends with popular people."

"No! I am unable to recall him,"

Haana postured towards him, her focus shifted from basket-ball game to Kunal,

"Why don't you sit?"

"Oh yes!" he sat down.

"So, what else that guy told you?"

"Nothing he boasted about his contact with celebs and told me about his friend who owns a Ferrari. I have once heard from you too that your friend owns a Ferrari, so I thought you must be knowing him. I told him I had no idea about a Ferrari in Delhi. All that I knew of the most expensive car in the city was Lamborghini owned by Sikander, the social media swagger."

"Yes! Sikander has that. He is one of the biggest entrepreneurs and investors we have in the city. I have met him a few times, he is a nice person but…"

Haana looked anxiously at Kunal and asked, "But?"

"But I have heard things that jeopardise his character."

"Would you mind sharing?"

"Nothing but his involvement with girls… after all he is rich, handsome and gravitating girls towards him would not be a big task."

"What do you mean? It's not bad if he is in a relationship."

"Not that way! Also, I have heard he has forcefully captured lands in the outskirts of the city which is a crime."

"Are you serious?"

"Yes"

"Did you see him doing all this?"

"No! How will I see this?"

"Then how can you believe in it?"

"I have come to know about this from my friends who know Sikander."

"Look! Saying words like he is involved with girls in another way about someone is not a good thing. I don't know him personally and neither do you, so it's not right to believe in what you have heard. And I can say that he can never be such a man."

She stood up, took her bag and said, "And yes, Sikander is successful, and people might envy his success and could have spread rumour like this to belittle him."

"Arey! I don't know actually, I told you what I have heard, I am not sure whether he is such a man or not."

"That's okay! But saying things like these about someone is not relevant which are nothing but 'Sootro ke Anusaar'

#

Haana was coming back to her class upstairs, when all the way she has been thinking, why did she defend Sikander before Kunal? Kunal could be right, after all he had met him several times, his friends were also involved with him but she had never even met Sikander. If Kunal was right, then why did she so confidently stand for Sikander? A natural reaction, she couldn't hear about him. However, Haana knew that though she didn't know Sikander personally, she still was sure that he couldn't be the kind of man Kunal had spoken. It was her heart that told her, gave clarifications for Sikander as Haana did not have logic to defend him because they have never met but her intuition loudly said Sikander was pure as she knew her intuition was her superpower, which had been guiding her all through. She dumped Kunal's words and genuinely had no after-effect too.

16

Catch up with Miss Shalini at CCD

2 days later, Haana received a call from Miss Shalini, the same lady who visited her college. She informed Haana that she had been selected by her and that she would like to meet her in person for further discussion. Haana told her that she could catch up with her on the coming Sunday only as she had other classes on the weekdays. Both agreed for Cafe Coffee Day.

Haana called Goher and informed her about her upcoming meeting with Miss Shalini, on which Goher laughed and said, 'She is trapping you, after the meeting she will keep a business proposal before you and ask you to invest a certain amount, it's better we hang out.'

Haana gave it a thought that what Goher said might be correct, so to check the authenticity of the lady she called three other students who were in top five and she couldn't call the other one as she did not know who that person was and from which department. On talking to them, she came to know that one of them was called on Monday.

Haana was confused whether to meet her or not, but, then she decided to take a leap of faith and go. She anticipated the circumstances, the most Miss Shalini could do was offer an investment which Haana had all rights to deny and if that did not happen, she could hopefully learn something from her.

It was Sunday. Haana went to CCD, parked her car and went inside where she saw the lady waiting for her. They looked at each other, shook hands and smiled. Being a good host, she asked Haana to be comfortably seated .
Soon the waiter arrived to take the order.
"What will you have?" Miss Shalini asked.
"A chocolate shake with ice cream."
"And you Ma'am?" The waiter asked.
"A cappuccino."
"I like your top," she complimented Haana.
"Oh! Thank You!"
"I guess I have seen it somewhere."
"Max! You might have seen it in one of the outlets of Max, I have got it from there."
"Haan! might be."
The waiter arrived and served the cappuccino to Miss Shalini and chocolate shake to Haana.
"Thank you, sir!" Haana said to the waiter.
Miss Shalini asked her, "So, Miss Writer, what do you write about?"

As she took her first sip of the chocolate shake, when her cheeks went inside and eyes got open on listening to 'Miss Writer,' Haana asked, "How do you know that I usually write?"
Miss Shalini smiled and said, "Social media ka zamana hai dost," and took the first sip.
Haana told her there was nothing specific, however, she had written poetries, short stories and also columns for renowned newspapers of the country. The lady told Haana that she resembled one of her friends and she would appreciate if Haana could recite any of her poem or tell a story.

Haana genuinely appreciated the interest that Miss Shalini showed towards her as an audience. Therefore, she proceeded with the very first poem that she wrote during her school days.

I said, he loves me,
They said, he is lying.
They said, forget him,
I said, I am trying.
He sounds so true, when he says he loves me too.
I laugh like a baby,
When I see him behaving crazy.
I feel so comfortable, when he rests on my shoulder,
As if a battle has been won by a soldier.
At the end of the day, I came to a conclusion,
Why do I love him enormously is still a confusion?

Miss Shalini clapped for her, pulled herself closer to pat Haana on her shoulder. Haana felt like a successful writer for the first time. It was the very first time she recited her poetry to someone other than her family and friends. Miss Shalini liked her poetry so much that she further insisted Haana to narrate one of her short stories too. However, Haana did not remember as she wrote them long time back.

Meanwhile the waiter showed up again with a smiling face, "Anything else, Ma'am?"

"A brownie please," Miss Shalini demanded.

"No! Thank You!" Haana apologised, as the waiter looked towards her.

"Yes! so please tell me any story that you have written," Shalini asked.

"I don't remember."

"Acha! Recall once."

Haana saw the interest in Miss Shalini's eyes and her body language as well, she gave her undivided attention. Haana too did not want to break her heart, therefore, out of nowhere she said to Miss Shalini, "I am writing a book; however, it's not yet complete."

Either she thought of it as the best excuse to give to Miss Shalini or her praises and attention gave her the courage to become an author, an instant decision.

"I have all the time and interest to listen to your story, I feel blessed to be listening to hopefully one of the biggest authors of the future," She responded.

Haana smiled and continued with her and Sikander's story, how she saw Sikander at Cafe Bronze, her feelings towards him, his mixed signals, tarot card session, how she met him on his birthday when she started dreaming about him and the dream happened to be a reality the following morning, her planning to gift him an expensive watch, planning for a secret party but how she saw him with his girlfriend, was a surprise for herself. She has described every situation and circumstances as it happened.

Miss Shalini was sitting on the couch as if she was sitting in her drawing room, both her legs were on the couch, one folded over the other and her face resting on both of her palms which was balanced by the elbow over the table.

Haana suddenly stopped.

"What happens next?"

"Next, even I don't know, haven't yet thought about the climax."

"Omg! Why? It's so interesting your characters, plot, story, everything."

"Thank You! I appreciate it."

"... The rest in underway, I would appreciate if you read it once it's published."

"I would love to," Miss Shalini replied.

Haana changed the topic and asked her about the reason behind their meeting, Miss Shalini told her to join her start-up company as a full-time content writer. Haana told her that she would love it, however, as she was pursuing her masters, she couldn't take break from her studies.Miss Shalini understood but suggested her to complete her story and get it published as she loved it and she believed that she could become a successful author.

#

The next day. Haana discussed about the event to her family. Told them how she narrated a story to Miss Shalini that she had been thinking of from sometime. Haana was encouraged by her family and she decided to complete the draft and find a good publisher for herself.

When Haana sat down to write the rest of her story, she wondered how she had no plans of becoming a writer but then she was working towards being an author. Had she hadn't met Miss Shalini she wouldn't have gotten a real time response from an audience and she wouldn't have known that she was a good storyteller. She thanked herself for the first time that she listened to her inner voice rather than following Goher's suggestion who advised her not to go and meet her in person. Haana knew that there was no way to look back, she wanted to become an author. She remembered what the monk told her in Bangkok, that situation would unfold naturally to her. All that she had to do was to follow her intuition. She had already attracted miracle in her life as Sikander, their meeting was no less than a miracle. Therefore, she decided to complete her story.

She wrote all about her journey, right from meeting Sikander, finding him on Social Media, enquiring about him, transforming herself to a better version.

Haana also wrote about one of the incidents which she did not exactly know, however, she considered it as an omen. A dream that introduced Sikander's girlfriend to Haana much before she was introduced by the universe in her real life. Where Haana saw Sikander with a girl visiting her place, wearing a black leather jacket and denim.

63

She was introduced to her by Sikander. When Sikander and her girl offered Haana a trip, she turned down the proposal and let both of them go together.

After a couple of days, Haana once again saw the same girl standing in a boutique. Interestingly, when Haana came to know about his girl from her social media account, she found out that this girl was a fashion designer.

Haana mentioned all about her journey, he transformation because of Sikander. She wrote that, *'Sikander was not her LOVE, but her STORY.'*

17

Still Something Missing at Cafe Bronze?

MARCH 2018

Kavya came back to Delhi after her trip to Chandigarh where she went to interview a famous Indian celeb. She had been making plans to catch up with Haana since a week, but failed. One final day, their stars matched and out of no surprise, Kavya asked her to meet at Cafe Bronze.

'Once again…?' Haana thought.

Haana went to see her. It was afternoon, but the weather was pleasant and beautiful, music was moderate, water was coming out of small fountain located at every third seat, fragrance was pleasant, yet something was missing, the place seemed incomplete. Haana sneaked in to look for Sikander (in case she was lucky) but she didn't.

Kavya got her bumps on the seat where Haana and she sat for the first first time.

Haana too took her royal seat, where she looked no less than a queen and saw her king Sikander, the first time. She settled down, took a deep breath and somehow consoled herself mentally to spend forty-five minutes there, forgetting the flashback and her story that brought her so far.

Kavya ordered tea, tried to hand over the menu card to Haana to continue with her order when she saw Haana looking at her with a smile but was lost somewhere.

"Haana, Haanaaaa" she called her and then she shook her yet there was no response. She was like time-lapsed.

"Are you there?" Kavya called out once again.

Haana looked at her, "Red Bull for me with white sauce pasta and French fries."

Kavya continued to chat, Haana kept on listening when she saw the white shirt, blue denim, tight half-open chest, and head bent down on his phone, who could be so stylish yet proud to isolate himself together with being an attention seeker. He was Sikander passing by the passage. For the first time in life, Haana smiled mentally (if at all one can smile this way.)

Her Red Bull wasn't even served, but she already got the wings. She was too high.

"Wo agaya dekho, dekho wo agayaaa."

Her mind immediately played the track, it's before she would shout 'Piya tu ab to aaja' she controlled herself, two more round of Sikander's walk, she would fly. She then saw Sikander leaving.

"Akele akele kaha ja rahe ho?"

That time she wanted to ask Sikander, she was trying to send some mental signals to Sikander 'stop, don't go' just like Rohit sends to call Jadoo in Koi Mil Gaya but Haana was not as genius as Rohit, she couldn't stop Sikander.

"Nature's Call," Haana stood up in vain, showed her rinky finger to Kavya and rash outside towards the washroom.

Her eyes searched for him everywhere but failed to find any trace of him. But she didn't want Kavya to know that she was looking for Sikander, so, she went to the washroom so that she wouldn't be caught for telling lies.

Failing to find Sikander, she came back and sat down, her mood was worsened that time. All her energy was drained out, even Red Bull failed to boost her up.

Then, once again Haana had to pass her time somehow, she had to listen all that Kavya had to boast about her trip to Chandigarh, but it didn't interest her at all.

Haana was being a good host and serving white sauce pasta to Kavya, meanwhile the plate was still in her hand, she looked straight and saw Sikander talking to a man, facing Haana, however, he was too proud if not shy to directly look at her, but was smiling as he already saw her.

"Haana, plate. Plate Haana," Kavya screamed.

"Haan," Haana kept it gently on the table, her battery was again 100% charged,

"When did he come, when I was in the washroom?" Haana muttered, with her first finger above her chin and her eye balls in the extreme left corner, making some unnecessary calculations.

"You look weird!" Kavya opinionated.

"I am sorry, was thinking something important."

She looked back at Sikander, but he vanished soon after. Her eyes went to the exit, where she saw Sikander leaving with the guy.

18

Most Expensive Shopping

Haana was very excited because she understood why her catch up plan had been delaying since a week. The universe planned a sneaky meeting with Sikander. The weather and Sikander directly affected her, she felt fresh and happy. As a token of love, she decided to take Kavya for shopping. They went to the shopping mall nearby, meanwhile, Haana was searching for the four-wheeler parking, while Kavya indicated by saying - 'That Way.'

"Are you sure? Nowhere it's written."

"Yes! I have been here so many times, we always park here."

The two girls went inside but when they came back after an hour, Haana's beautiful red car was missing. She was shocked, she couldn't accept the absence of her car. Her hands went cold.

To make sure, she searched in other directions too, but she didn't find it. A drop of sweat fell from her forehead down her cheeks. Her heart was pounding and she could feel her body shaking and sweating at the same time. She turned back and yelled, "Kavya, where is my car?"

"We left it here, right?" Kavya had a fishy face, she too was tensed, rather she looked composed (after all it wasn't her car.)

Haana noticed Kavya talking to the man who was the security guard-cum-bill checker at the exit. The man seemed more like traffic police who was directing Kavya with his hands. Haana couldn't understand anything so, she went to the two-in-one guy and asked him to repeat all that he told to Kavya.

He told her, that her car was taken away by the Palika. 'Paalika?' Haana questioned herself. She remembered she has been to Paalika Bazaar some 6-7 years back. Her thought was interrupted when she heard, 'Nagar Nigam Paalika.'

"How do you know our car has been taken there?" Kavya asked.

"Our car?" Haana thought 'when did I give her the ownership.' Nevertheless, the important issue was how could she get back the car?

Two-in-one replied, "All the cars that are parked here at no-entry are taken there."

"When you knew this, why didn't you inform us before?" Haana shouted in a mild tone

"Madame hume ka pata tha, gaadi aapki hai?" he answered.

(How would I know, it's your car?)

"How will we reach there?" Haana asked in a panic.

The next few moments, the security informed Haana about how could she retrieve her car from the Nagar Palika's captivity. Though it seemed to be a too stressful job, she had to get her car anyway.

\#

Haana ran down the stairs, she forgot she had a friend left behind but that didn't matter her as she was the defaulter. The last two steps, Haana jumped and ran towards the auto-rickshaw. When the rickshaw driver saw them running towards him, he was sure he was about to get some business and said, "Baithye baithye."

"Nagar Nigam Chalna hai na?" he asked.

(We have to go to the Nagar Nigam's office)

The two girls looked at each other amazingly, they have the same question on their face, which Haana finally asked, "Aapko kaise pata?"

(How do you know?)

The driver laughed sarcastically and said, "Arey Madame, Bhaagte Jhole, udhte baal aur pareshan chehre ke saath log wahe jaane ke lie aate hain."

Haana looked straight at the road and saw a crane dragging a red car, she assumed it as her. For the first time, she felt a sense of motherhood in her heart. Seeing your child ruthlessly being dragged by a crane before your eyes was not a pleasant experience. Tears filled her eyes, everything appeared magnifying to her, she controlled hard not to let it fall and she succeeded that time.

"Pareshan mat hoye," the driver comforted.

(Don't Worry)

"Just pay them Rs.500 and make sure they don't make the receipt," he continued.

(The further communication took place in Hindi)

"Rs.500? Are you sure? I have heard of Rs.1100 Rs fine imposed in India. Will they agree?" Haana asked.

"Of course! You want your car, they want money," he confidently answered.

"Hmmm," Kavya interrupted.

"Once again make sure, they don't make the receipt, else it will go to govt records."

As the auto rickshaw stopped, Haana jumped out of it, she did not even bother to pay the driver, Kavya was there to take care of it.

Haana walked towards the booth of the Nagar Nigam. When she saw her red, beautiful, sizzling kid standing all safe at the left side of the road, she closed her eyes, took a deep breath and was thankful for its safety. Kavya paid the driver and rushed towards Haana who had already reached the booth, which had a small net window.

Haana bent down to request. Meanwhile, Kavya bumped into her in vain.

"Seedhe khade raho," Haana annoyingly replied.

The friend who was a guest 15 minutes before is now a liability to Haana.

Kavya apologised.

Haana looked inside and said the three magical words, "Sir Meri Gadi…"

(Sir my car…)

The man inside pointed his palm outside the booth.

Haana came back to her posture, moved beside the booth where she saw a police officer standing who just finished his lunch and was accompanied by a laid who was pouring water from a jug to help him wash his hands. After the officer washed his hands, he asked the boy for the jug, pour some water in his mouth and played with it inside.

At first, he rolled his mouth, then he washed all the bacteria inside, opened it, looked up made some indifferent voice aaaa… kaaaaa….grrr…aathuuuu

Haana was already stressed, on top of it, the officer's Swacha Bharat Abhyan was not coming to an end. And finally, he spat it. Haana found it very funny, but in such a crucial situation, even smiling was unaffordable to her.

The officer looked at her and she looked back to explain. When the officer too showed his hand and directed her without opening his mouth to talk to the people inside. Haana was unable to understand why the officer who took 2-3 minutes to clean his Taj Mahal inside, did not utter a word but pointed. Was he too conscious of the hard work that he had done and did not want to open his mouth so that the germs would go? Whatever! She bent again and approached the man she first saw in the booth. She saw two men coming from the same auto-rickshaw in the same position the driver described of victims.

She looked back at the man inside who looked at these two men, then asked Haana to sit in her car, he will get back to her after 10 minutes.

19

Drama of a Red Lifted Car

Haana and Kavya stepped towards the car, as Haana opened the door, she kissed the top of the door and held it for a few seconds, that motherly hug. Haana was about to discuss how to cope up with the situation, when Kavya spoke, "Isn't it too hot?"

Haana stared at her and thought that at first place she got her car picked up by the Nagar Nigam and made her go through all those experience and then she was even feeling hot. Where has she landed from Chandigarh or Canada? Then the other side of her made her recall that Kavya too underwent all that experience with her. Also, she took directions from the security guard, then she paid to the auto-rickshaw driver. Not that bad.

Haana switched on the air conditioner. Kavya said in a formal tone, "Arey! It's okay. It's manageable."

'No unnecessary formalities. That's what you intended, so I did' - she shouted in her mind.

The cold temperature made them relax and to think of better ideas. Kavya opened her wallet, took out 10 notes of Rs.100 and gave it to Haana.

Haana did not understand it. Kavya explained her to give that to the officer inside when he would summon them.

Haana was touched, she told her that she too had a two thousand rupee note.

But then, she remembered that the auto-rickshaw driver said he would charge five hundred rupees, but legally in India, the penalty amount was one thousand and one hundred rupees. What if she pays him her a two hundred rupee note and he would charge rupees one thousand and one hundred only, rather than five hundred rupees. Or, what if he does not return any money? No! Bad idea.

So, she took those ten notes of hundred rupees each from Kavya and very smartly divided it into two parts with five in each. She kept five hundred rupees in her wallet and gave the other five notes to Kavya.

"Why are you returning?" Kavya asked with her brows joined in curiosity

"Keep it, I will come back and take it if I need. If I take all the money, I have to pay all," she replied.

"But but…" Kavya tried to speak,

"Asta Lavista Baby," Haana said this and shut the door of the car.

#

She came to the officer and said what she was made to remember like a Ratto Tota by the autorickshaw driver,

"Sir jo paise pade lelo lekin receipt mat kaato."

(Take the money but don't make the receipt)

"No Madame! Not possible."

"Sir please sir, try to understand."

"Madame, you try to understand."

"Sir, if you make the receipt, my details would go to government records."

The officer laughed and said, "That's why we are sitting here."

"It's the very first time, something happened like this, and I don't want my details to go to the government records."

"Don't Worry! Nothing will happen. Ghar pe receipt nahi jayegi."

(The receipt will not be sent to your home)

"That's not an issue sir, please understand."

"Five hundred rupees sir, no receipt please, look at my face."

"Five hundred only?" his face had the secret mark of asking, "Are you trying to bribe a government servant for five hundred rupees only?"

"One thousand rupees only, Madame."

Madame smartly used her trick, opened her wallet and took out the five notes,

"Sir! This is all I have," a victim lying along with proof.

"No Madam," he denied the negotiation.

"Alright! Let me get it then," the trick failed. Haana went to Kavya and offered her palm before her. Kavya gave her remaining five hundred rupees.

Haana gave the money to the officer, when a mixed voice of gutka and spit comes from beside, "Driving License dijiye," the local man asked.

'Hai Ma! Matajiiiiii. Ye kya maang lia' Haana told to herself.

Had he asked her hand for his son, would have sounded better; or, even her kidney but, 'Inhone to direct driving License he maang liya.'

All that time whatever Haana tried controlling seemed unbearable. She could burst anytime. However, she knew to negotiate with them was nothing but a waste of time. It was better to provide and so she did. Haana looked at him and asked, "Will you return it?"

"Yes of course, just let me note down your license number once."

"Please, don't write it."

The first officer interrupted, "Aha! Don't worry."

"Pitaji tak baat nahi pahuchege."

Haana knew that they thought Haana was scared because the news could reach her place, however, Haana always shared everything with her parents and she had always been her daddy's girl.

"Pitaji ko to sabse pehle main he bataunge."

"Arey wah madame! Yeh baat aapki hume bohat ache lage, Pitaji se kabhe kuch nahi chupana chahye."

"Ache lage to number mat note karye," she conversed to the officer when the local officer who had asked for the driving license returned her license and confirmed, "Isse baat pe aapki, driving number nahi note kia, yeh lijiye."

Haana smiled the most expensive and painful smile in her life.

However, it was a fair deal, they made the receipt but did not note her license number.

20

An Unwelcomed Appearance

AUGUST 2018

Haana was lying on her bed in her loose pyjamas, watching the television, eating Lay's Magic Masala and still getting bored. No more plans to hang out with any friends as the last outing had already cost her a lot. Suhaana walked into the room.

"What are you doing?" she asked. Haana ignored her.

"I asked you something, I guess!"

"Shall I give you the number?" Haana asked.

"Whose number?"

"Optometrist. Oh! I mean eye specialist. Can't you see from your big round eyes that I am chilling."

"Lying like a crocodile and eating like a buffalo is what you call chilling?"

"Shut the door when you leave."

"I came here to inform you that your bad days are coming."

Haana gave her a side look, stood on the bed with folded knees, blinked her eyes continuously and asked in a gentle mind tone, "Why? What happened? Anything wrong?"

"Unbelievable, is it the same girl I tried to communicate with a few seconds back?"

Haana kept on blinking and gave the most innocent expression she could ever make.

"Chakotra is coming. Mom asked me to inform you. She has a seven-day plan to attend some wedding and tomorrow she will be here with us for the next three days."

"You mean she is already in the city from last three days?" Haana rolled her eyeballs, and went straight back flat on the bed and shouted, "Oh! No"

#

Haana met Pummy Aunty in the year 2014, an O-shaped lady somewhere in her mid-forties from Jaipur, chubby cheeks with no dimple chin. Irrespective of the number of years, she has taken around the sun, she still treated herself as a twenty-year-old girl. Women compete with women with regards to ageing but she competed with girls half her age. They first met when Haana visited the Pink City for her vacation to her uncle's place. She was her uncle's neighbour. A loving lady with no kids, her husband was a textile entrepreneur, the only breadwinner of the family who earned for his fat chick to spend. The duo justified their job. Though, she was not like a typical 'padosi' (neighbour) who always asked for 'sugar' or 'salt.' However, she was annoying, interfering and a big hypocrite. If ever she found someone wearing a new dress, the first thing that would come out of her mouth was, "How much did it cost you?"

"I have the same dress."

She liked to indulge her nose in everyone's business to find out what the other person was up to.

Haana described Pummy Aunty to Suhaana when she came back home, and they had named her "Chakotra" which referred to the after-effect of the dung of an insect, a poisonous effect.

But what makes her tolerable to Haana was the fact that Pummy Aunty had tremendous respect for Haana's Mom. The two ladies first met when Mrs Qadri (Haana's Mom) came to fetch Haana from her uncle's place. Moreover, Pummy Aunty was kind and affectionate, she was an amazing cook, whenever she cooked anything she always sent it for Mom and Haana. Till date, Mrs Qadri and Pummy Aunty have been in touch.

21

Moori Moments

Early morning at 5:45 am, Haana woke up, looked at the wall clock and tried to figure out the reason behind the fact that she woke up so early. The bad thing was that she woke up fresh, so she couldn't sleep any further. She saw a crow resting at her balcony and was speaking in his language "Cawww-Cawww." The sound of the crow was initially funny but eventually became unpleasant to her. Haana thought another omen that Chakotra was coming. The universe was sending her a message in the form of a crow about her arrival. The mind travels faster than light. Immediately, Haana's mind took her to Sikander, omen, universe, synchronicities and soon these terms juggled in her mind. She dropped them, jumped out of her bed and went inside the kitchen to make herself a cup of tea. She poured the water, milk and sugar into a pan and let it boil for three minutes. After that, she added tea which changed the colour of the mixture immediately.

"Do I have to wake up early morning for three days to prepare tea for Pummy Aunty? Waking up early morning, especially for Chakotra, no way! This lady is going to give me sleepless nights," Haana talked to herself.

Meanwhile, the bell rang and she went to open the door.

"Subah Subah kaun bell bajata hai?"(Who knocks at the door early morning?)

She peeped into the key-hole in the doorknob to see who was on the other side. When she did not find anyone, she returned and picked the newspaper which was lying on the floor. Going through the headlines, she smelled something, she inhaled and exhaled repetitively to make sure whether something was smelling or it was just her nose playing games. She remembered her tea was on the flame. She threw the newspaper on the centre table and ran towards the kitchen.

The tea had frothed and fallen onto the kitchen floor but a handsome quantity was still in the pan. Haana poured the tea in her big mug to take it with moori and call that delicious combination as "chai-moori." Haana came to know about "moori" from one of her juniors in college who was a Bengali, whom Haana saw eating this on their college tour in graduation days. Haana told her that she knew about "Jhaal-muri," "Bhel-moori" but what is "chai moori"? On asking her she explained it was "moori," which is also called 'puffed rice' good for the mind and that's what Bengali children usually ate during the exam as it is believed to sharpen one's mind. Also, Haana showed her interest in eating that just like her junior was eating. The girl told Haana that it was very simple, all she had to do was to mix moori with tea. Haana tried it for the first time and from that day, she eats chai moori daily for breakfast.

Haana mostly enjoys that combination at morning time, where there was no one to disturb her. Many times, before, she had tired it in the evening time also, however, people's reaction had been strange on mixing moori with chai. Also, Haana had been criticised on her diet as it was daunting for people to accept that such a slim and fit girl could eat so much moori with tea. Therefore, to avoid such criticism she enjoyed her moori moments in solitude.

#

She took the mug and her big air-tight container of moori which was beside the fridge and proceeded towards the balcony. She soon realised that she had forgotten the spoon to eat with. She went back to the dining room, took the spoon and her smartphone from her bedroom and came back to the balcony. She sat down, with her leg overlapped by the other, mug in her hand, mobile on the swing and container on her lap.

"Cawwww-Cawww," once again the crow sought attention. "I know Chakotra is coming and I am prepared, now kindly leave," Haana said that to the crow with both her hands joined, having the tea mug in between.

As she said that, the crow flew.

"My God! Does it mean he was here for me; anyway, I don't get this universal language of communication."

Haana took out a palm-full of moori with her hand and put it into the tea, making sure that not even a single piece of puffed rice fell to the ground. She knew the maid would complain to her Mom if the floor was dirty and she would get to hear a good yelling. She closed the container, kept it down beside the swing and mixed the moori with the spoon. Then, she noticed that 3-4 pieces of moori were on the floor which she collected and kept on her phone which was on her lap. Suddenly she noticed the time on her phone which said 06:06 hours. She frowned and recalled how she had been seeing angel numbers 11:11 last night and other such numbers from last 3-4 months. Every time her eyes caught those numbers, she immediately googled it. Some numbers conveyed a message of miracles, some had the meaning of soul mate manifestation like 02:02 and other numbers had respective meaning. However, that time she ignored the indication '06:06 hours.'

22

Happy Publishing

After she was done having moori with tea, she got an email notification in her phone. She quickly opened it and was too excited to see it. She screamed out loud, out of happiness and started hopping across the balcony and went inside her parents' bedroom without even knocking at the door. Her excitement made her senseless, she went inside like a kangaroo and shouted, "Dada (Papa), Mumyyyyy."

"What happened, what happened?" the duo asked with curiosity.

Mummy jumped out of bed and checked her out from head to toe.

"What Happened?" Mom asked.

"What happened?" Haana asked.

"Are you okay? Did a nail get inside your feet or something heavy fell on it? Sit down first," Mom said with concern.

Dad was asking Mom to finish first so that he can ask the very same question,

"What happened?

She bit her lips and first, she looked at her mom and then at her dad. Finally, she stopped hopping.

She realised that her mom & dad were worried listening to her shouting, they might be wondering why did she shout and at the first place how she was awake so early, so that reaction of theirs was natural.

"Ohkeeyyy," she closed her eyes and joined her hands.

She jumped on the bed and offered her phone to her Dad directly and asked him to read out with a big smile on her face. Ironically, the very first thing that was offered to Dad was a mobile phone with an open mail instead of a cup of tea.

"Will anybody tell me what is going on," Mom asked.

"Give me my glasses," Dad asked for them.

It's before Mummy could pass it, Haana hurriedly jumped and picked it before Mom.

"uhmm...hmmm.., pagal he hue jarahen hain."(Going crazy)

She gave to Dada, he wore it and read.

Meanwhile, Mom was curious but after looking at Dad and then the phone, she knew it wouldn't be wise to ask Haana anything more because it wouldn't fetch her answers as she had already lost her mind.

After a minute, Dad looked at Mom, from his glasses, raised his brow and said

"Your daughter is soon going to be an author."

He landed comfortably back to his posture, covered his face with the quilt and asked Haana to explain further.

"You remember Mom? I have sent my manuscript to one of the biggest publishers of India, they have notified me today that they are ready to publish my book. So, I have to travel to Mumbai tomorrow as they are based in Mumbai."

Mom smiled. Her eyes were full of tears and that motherly feeling emerged, however, she did not cry.

Haana looked at her phone, gave a wide smile like never before, hugged her phone and said, "Finally, I don't have to accompany Pummy Aunty anymore."

Mom looked at Haana surprisingly, a dual expression of vanishing tears and anger appeared on her face, she asked her, "So, I thought you are genuinely happy because of this mail but are you excited just because you don't have to accompany Chakotra, I mean Mrs Pummy?

The bed was shaking, dad was laughing inside his quilt.

23

Raju Ban Gaya Gentleman

SEPTEMBER 2018

The car stopped, the door opened, a lady stopped at the entrance. Finally, Pummy aunty was there. Haana's eyes caught her legs at first where she saw Chakotra wearing gents' sports shoe or it was too loose for her. Her leggings made her legs even more fat, than skinny. On top of it, she was wearing a loose kurta which was the only so-called eligible outfit on her torso coupled with a decent chiffon scarf. Her left hand had a beautiful wristwatch with stones embodied on, therefore, it was daunting for Haana to figure out whether it was a diamond watch or it was a mere stone one. The right hand was full of bangles, more than a new bride would wear. Her hair was neatly tied in a simple ponytail. Her face which merged with the neck had basic day makeup, therefore, none could say where the face ended or the neck started. So to overcome that problem, a shiny gold chain was rolled around her neck, which was shiny enough to grab one's attention from far and hence acted as a borderline more than jewellery.

Chakotra smiled and further came in, greeted Mrs Qadri at first, then Haana with a warm hug and some unnecessary wet kisses. Later she gestured towards Suhaana. Dada already left for work so Chakotra could only meet him at dinner.

#

The round dining table was arranged. Everyone was seated. Dad and Pummy Aunty had exchanged a few words. Mom had already made the necessary preparations, the maid was only to serve the hot, yummy food over the table. Suhaana and Pummy Aunty were discussing something very unimportant when Dad enquired Haana: "Ready to fly?"
Haana excitedly replied, "Yes! Dada, all packed."
Suhaana was unaware of the whole situation, "Where are you flying?"
To add more spice to the situation, she further added: "Pummy aunty is here and you are talking about leaving somewhere."
Chakotra, like always was very curious and before she could ask anything, as a proud mother of the budding author, Mom told her about the whole situation. Pummy Aunty congratulated her.
"So, who are you going with?" Chakotra asked.
"Your niece is a big girl now, Aunt. I will take care of myself," Haana replied with a fake smile
"NA-BABA-NA" Chakotra uttered these words, further, "You can't trust anyone these days Mrs Qadri, sending a girl to an all-new big city like Mumbai is not a safe option."
An angry expression took over Haana's face, she bit her lips and looked at Chakotra. The spoon stand on the table also had a knife, Haana was analysing its sharpness for a murder.
"Why don't you take Pummy aunty along, Haana?" Suhaana suggested.

"You have three days in Delhi, aunty, and you have already seen the places, Mumbai would be a new experience, you never know, stars would be in your favour and you might get to see your favourite star "Shah Rukh Khan," Suhaana completed with all her teeth out, leaving no way for Haana to escape.

On hearing Shah Rukh's name, Pummy aunty got enormously excited, felt nostalgic and told Suhaana about her resemblance to Juhi Chawla. To make the situation worse, Suhaana exclaimed, "Oh Really? Wow!"

"You know beta, when we were in college, I went to watch Raju Ban Gaya Gentleman with my friends, by mistake I sat on someone else seat. The boy came to me and said- "Oh Juhi Chawla apne seat pe baitho."

Suhaana had no idea how to control herself from laughing. To play safe she covered her mouth with her palm, and her hand resting on the table, which would appear to Chakotra as if she was listening. She looked at Haana and gave her a dying expression with her neck bent right side and her tongue out. Haana went red. That time she was thinking about two murders with one knife.

Dada too was trying to avoid the situation as controlling laughter for him was a not an easy task. Haana pulled her chair to leave when Dad looked at her and signalled her from his eyes to sit, his calm expression conveyed to Haana that he would take care of her.

"Yes! this would be nice, if Mrs Pummy would accompany Haana to Mumbai, we too would be in relief that someone is there to take care of her," Mom appreciated Pummy aunty's sense of warmth and love towards Haana.

"Yes! That would have been great however the tickets are already booked," Dad made a sad face when a smile after a long time appeared on Haana's face.

"Tickets aren't yet booked, she was booking online but her card showed some technical error, she was waiting for you to come so that she can use your card," Mom revealed it.

"What a piece of art she is?" Dad silently muttered.

"I think even God wanted Mrs Pummy to go with Haana," Suhaana added

Haana's eyes were filled with tears.

24

Picture Abhi Baaki hai Mere Dost

The dinner was over, Dad came into his room, Haana followed her and banged the door.

"Dada, what is happening? We had no plans with Pummy Aunty."

It's before Dad could reply, a "chrrrr" voice came, the door was half-opened by Suhaana, whose face was visible and the whole body was out in the dining.

"Shall we come in?"

"UGHHH," Haana closed her palms and sat behind Dad with her head resting on his shoulder.

"Kindly come in, Pummy Aunty" Suhaana invited her in

"I was thinking why to waste time, so I came to help Haana with the reservations, she can use my card for payment," Suhaana replied sarcastically.

"Beta, at least ask Aunty, she has to seek permission from her husband, and whether she has time or not." Dad gave it a last try to cut off Chakotra from the program that she tried to fit in.

"Oh! Bhaisahab, it's okay, Haana is a daughter to me, I would love to accompany her, Chakotra protested in a better way.

First flight for tomorrow from DELHI to MUMBAI, Suhaana typed on Dad's system

'First Flight? what a b#### she is!' Haana abused her in mind.

#

Her dream of "solo-travelling" to the City of Dreams was broken. The first-time solo experience that she might have got to encounter was already not about to happen. She was not unhappy because she couldn't go alone but what made the situation worse was the fact that all her trip will be ruined by Chakotra, airport, flight, hotel, city, airport, flight............. Intolerable.

Haana had a two-day plan in Mumbai. The first day, Haana had to meet the publishers and then she had to attend an event organised by them. The second day for contract signing. Initially, she had a three-day program, where one day for travelling the city, however, that wasn't imaginable with Chakotra by her side, so it was better to go for two days - less time, less wastage of energy.

#

Day 1
Landing on the City of Dreams & Meeting the Dream

The flight departed at 8:30 am and arrived at Chattrapati Shivaji Maharaj International Airport at 10:35 am. The two ladies checked in at the hotel. They freshened up and after almost an hour, Haana visited the publisher's office for the meeting, where she was told about the event that she was also invited for where one of the biggest business tycoons of the country was the guest speaker. She couldn't deny the invitation. She was surprised when she was told by her publishing manager Mr Shekhar that the venue of the event was the banquet of the same hotel where she was staying. Two hours had passed by, the conversations between Haana and Shekhar went on and on. Haana's publishing manager was originally from Delhi, which gave them some common things to share. He was a newly married man who shared his love story with Haana, talked about his professional and personal struggle, how it took him eight years to convince his in-laws, but at last how he succeeded both in his personal and professional life with due patience, devotion, and persistence. He thanked the city Mumbai for giving him all that he had.

"Do you believe that Mumbai gave you all this?"

"Yes of course!"

The spark in his eyes convinced Haana.

He further added, "I was a dreamer back then in Delhi, but ever since I came to Mumbai, I manifested my dreams. You never know Haana what this place has in store for you, you never know, your biggest dream too can come true. Years back Shah Rukh Khan stood at Bandstand and said: "One day I will be the King" and the world knows him as BADSHAH. He came here in search of his love but he discovered his purpose too."

"What Purpose?"

"Acting, what gave him everything - name, success, respect and whatnot."

Haana looked at him and observed the purity and honesty in his words which was a reflection of his experience. He continued, "I came here for my purpose & I met the love of my life. I read your manuscript and loved it, but as you mentioned by the law of attraction, synchronicity, and omens, I believe they are sent by the universe and are aligned.

"When your LOVE makes you discover your PURPOSE in LIFE, Or Your PURPOSE introduces you to your LOVE"

"Mine was the latter case, you have to explore which one is yours, you never know just like your character you too could meet your Real LIFE SIKANDER."
Welcome to the City of Dreams

25

An Invitation to the Event

Haana came back to her hotel where Chakotra was already waiting for her. Chakotra inquired Haana about her visit to the office. She informed her about the timing of the event and how co-incidentally it was taking place at their hotel itself.

#

The two ladies got ready and went to the hall where the event was organised. Haana was dressed in formals, dark brown trouser, half sleeves light brown shirt, a Michael Kors watch, simple round silver ear-rings and basic makeup. They entered and saw how perfectly everything was organised. Round tables were neatly arranged with white sheets and small flower pots were kept on every table. Each table had five chairs to sit. The yellow light was perfect for photography. A small water bottle was kept for everyone. As they both entered inside, Haana's eyes were searching for Mr Shekhar who was the only person she knew and her friend from the last five hours. She looked at the right side near the board where she saw him talking to a man whom she guessed to be the speaker of the evening, the business tycoon whom they came to hear, however, she could not see him as his back was facing her. Shekhar looked at her, smiled and shook his head which was a verbal message that he was coming, he signalled from his hand for her to sit.

Haana and Chakotra sat down, Chakotra was panicking for no reason and took the first sip from the bottle kept there.

"Hello Haana," Shekhar called. Haana turned back

Haana stood up for a formal handshake. Shekhar apologised for being late as he was busy with the speaker (Haana guessed it right) and then thanked Haana for joining them to the event and explained another reason why she was invited on that day in particular. Firstly, because the speaker's valuable words would be of great help to everybody present there and secondly he was also from Delhi.

Shekhar asked them to be seated comfortably as the event would start within 10 minutes.

26

The Destined Meeting

The host initiated the formal conversation and introduced the speaker by mentioning some of his achievements, background. Meanwhile, Haana was busy scrolling her social media feed and posts. When her ears heard the most heart-beating name "SIKANDER" she could hear the beat of her heart, she looked at CHAKOTRA surprisingly, who was very much involved with the program. She looked at the audience and saw a handsome man walking towards the stage, smartly dressed in a black tuxedo. He stood at the podium with a big smile on his face, the same smile that can make anyone fall for him. Haana's eyes were naturally filled with tears and why not, it was none other than Sikander, her Sikander.

Her body started shivering, a sense of anxiety took over her. For the first time, she was not excited but anxious to see him. Seeing her man in black tuxedo she thought how similar he looked to her fantasy proposal. Where she fantasised herself standing inside a beautiful open garden area, Sikander arriving in his luxurious car, stepping out of it with his black formal shiny shoes, killing in his black tuxedo, coming towards Haana looking at her, bending down on his knees and proposing for a life-long relationship [marriage]. All the secret photographer clicking their pictures. Haana surprisingly looks at him with tears in her eyes saying yes and then he lifts her but the reality was different, that time he did not give her butterflies but her heart started pounding.

Her three years journey, her crush story all flashed before her. She did not know how to react, whether she would be happy that destiny made them come together or sad as she knew they could never be together. Shekhar was sitting with them and had two other females on his other side also. He looked at Haana and asked if everything was okay with her. She assured him that she was alright and because of travelling, the changing weather the cold was taking over her, she felt like sneezing but she couldn't and that's why her eyes were watery.
She wasn't just a good writer but a good actor too.

Sikander was on with his speech and experiences, meanwhile, Haana was thinking about everything that happened in the last three years. The guy she wanted to hear, was talking, the man she wanted to know about once, was telling everything about himself, the face she couldn't forget was all time before her, yet, she could not get the courage to look at him and see him. She knew she behaved most indifferently that day. The event that she was excited about from the last two days ever since she came to know about it, was now a cage for her and she wanted to escape.

#

The event was over, Haana was about to leave when Mr Shekhar insisted her for dinner. She denied, told Mr Shekhar that she was full. Mr Shekhar looked at Pummy aunty and asked her for the same. Pummy aunty smiled and convinced Haana to leave after dinner. Meanwhile, Shekhar asked Haana to accompany her. She went to the dining hall where Mr Shekhar introduced Sikander to Haana.

The same expression gathered on their faces. They were expressionless. Sikander did not expect Haana and vice-versa. Mr Shekhar informed Haana that he was the great business tycoon, the speaker we have had the fortune to meet and listen to his experience. He also introduced Haana to Sikander, saying that 'she is an amazing writer and a budding author, we have the privilege of publishing a book. She too is from Delhi and is here for her book.'

They both smiled formally, none said a single word but nodded their head on each other's introduction.

Pummy aunty came with her plate of food, looked at Sikander and smiled.

"You are also from Delhi?" she asked.

"Yes," he replied with a smile.

For the first time, Haana properly heard him. Precisely, a 'yes' from him; if not for any other question.

Accidentally their eyes met for the first time in three years. They were standing before each other, undivided attention, they both were clear what they were looking at. Three years, the law of attraction worked, their accident meeting at Cafe Bronze, bumping into each other lives every time one tried to overlook the other, the mixed signals, stalking each other, making oneself better for the other, cry, sadness, happiness, enquiring about each other all lead them there. *'The Universe exactly lead them where they are destined to be.'*

27

Stomach Ache

FRIDAY 10:45 PM

The dinner was over. Haana did not eat anything but waited for Pummy aunty to finish on Shekhar's words. She could not see Sikander anywhere. She came back to her room.

Haana was on the bed thinking about the evening, Sikander's appearance, their meeting, his voice when she heard a painful voice, "Help Haana!"

She went to the washroom and saw Chakotra standing to vomit with her right hand on her fat belly, "What's wrong?"

"I over-ate and I want to vomit out but I can't. I got acidity too. Omg! Help me!"

"Oh! Wait, Shall I get you ENO?"

"Please."

Haana ran back, opened her luggage and took out her medicine pouch, which Mumma gave her to ensure that she suffers from no pain while travelling. It had a dettol, band-aid and all kinds of medicines but no ENO. Mom knew Haana would never over-eat.

Haana called the room service and asked them to send a sachet of ENO. She went back to the washroom and enquired about the current status of Chakotra.

"Same."

Haana asked her to sit on the couch, she did.

The doorbell rang,

"ENO is here Don't Worry," Haana said.

She opened the door and saw the boy with a sad expression as if he had practised it several times before coming. He bowed down his head, looked at the floor, hands joined below belt and said what Haana already feared about.

"Ma'am! Extremely sorry, we looked up but we don't have ENO here, It's late so we couldn't even get it from the nearby shop as they would be closed by now. Is there anything else that we could help you with?"

She nodded her head like an 8-year-old girl and immediately replied, "Nimbu Paani"

"No No," a voice came from inside. Chakotra dropped the idea of Nimbu Paani

"Lemon doesn't suit me."

Then she yelled from inside, "Such a big hotel, no ENO"?

The bell boy bit his lips and blinked his eyes.

Haana replied, "It's Okay, Thank You!"

She rolled her eyes and shut the door.

#

Five minutes later, there was a knock again. Haana opened it and saw the same bell boy with a packet of ENO, a glass of water covered with a coaster and a spoon on a small tray.

Her mouth was opened out of curiosity but the bell boy replied before she asked anything.

"When Ma'am expressed her inconvenience for the medicine availability at the hotel, the sir in the next room heard it while he was entering his room. Fortunately, he had it and he asked me to provide to you."

"How nice of him? Convey our gratitude to him," Haana smiled and received it.

As per the advertisement, it would take three minutes for ENO to show its effect, however, a big stomach like Chakotra was relieved within two minutes twenty-eight seconds.

"Was I too loud?" Chakotra asked Haana

Haana bit her lips and replied, "a little rude, doesn't matter aunty, you were in pain."

"Shall I apologise?" she asked.

"That would be sweet."

Haana went towards the landline to call the bell boy when she saw Chakotra leaving the room in the nightie. She went towards the gaming zone which was at the other side of the big corridor. Haana stood at the door, with her one leg draped over the other and her hands folded to see how Chakotra was going to apologise to the bell boy. Haana could see Chakotra standing at the billiard board, talking to someone, however, she could not see the bell boy or anyone that she was talking to. She was sure that it was not the bell boy that she was talking to, but who else? She was wondering all that when a shot took a movement on the board, and she could see SIKANDER standing in front of Chakotra. His palm rested on the billiard stick. She could see them talking to each other and smiling. When Sikander's eyes caught Haana, he directed Chakotra to her with his eyes. Chakotra waved a bye and Sikander smiled.

28

Crushing over CRUSH

Haana hurriedly came back to the room and sat down. Pummy aunty too rushed in. She closed the door with a loud bang. It was before Haana would ask anything, she initiated in excitement.

"I apologised" with both her palm twisting twice.

"When? I saw you talking to the guest speaker."

"Yes! I went to apologise to him."

"Him? For?"

"For I shouted, that was rude you said, right?.'

"Yes! But you yelled at the bell boy, I thought you were going to apologise to him."

"Bell Boy? Why would I apologise to him? It was Sikander, the same man who is staying in the room next to ours and sent us ENO."

"Sikander?"

"Yes! our guest speaker, that handsome boy, his name is Sikander."

"How do you know?"

"I also know he is some big businessman from Delhi, that's what he told down in his event to everyone."

"Oh Yes! I forgot, he was the guest speaker, told everything about him, I got it. I am sorry...so sorry. By the way, how do you know he is the same man who sent you ENO?"

"I asked him downstairs where are you staying, he told me the same hotel, so I asked for his room number. What a coincidence when he told me his room number, I told him ours was next to him. He is a wonderful man."

"Hmm!" Haana took a deep breath and looked and played with the corner of the pillow.

"He asked about you."

"MEEEh? Really? What did he ask?"

"He asked me how I was related to you."

Haana's eyes were wide open, she insisted on explaining word for word what he had said.

Chakotra looked at Haana doubtfully and replied, he asked: "How are you related to the author?"

Haana's mouth was open (she remembered how Sikander asked the same question to Aidh concerning how am I related to him.)

"Is that what he asked?"

"Yes! Why do you ask?"

"Casually,"

"So, what did you reply?"

"I told him that I am your aunt and I was accompanying you here. He is a nice man. I wish he was here until we leave, but he is leaving tomorrow."

"Is he?"

"Yes." Chkotra nodded in grief.

\#

Day 2
Saturday 11 am

Haana woke up and found Chakotra missing next to her on the bed, she went to the washroom to see if she was there but she wasn't. She got worried and called her. Her phone was ringing in the room itself, on the bed. Haana got tensed and inquired about a fat lady who was with her to the hotel staff. And then she saw four staff members carrying a stretcher towards her room. The patient was

Pummy aunty herself, covered with a white gown on top of her two-piece swimming suit. She was placed on the bed like a heavy showpiece with gentle care.

"Hawww, what happened"

The staff left.

"First, close the door," Chakotra whispered with one eye open

"Oh! Haana I cannot tell you what all happened," Chakotra replied delightfully.

Haana was shocked to hear that tone, she became nervous and asked suspiciously,

"What?"

Immediately Chakotra sat up, held Haana from both her hands and said, "Sikander, Sikander"

"Hain?" Haana was in chaos

"Oh! My my, Haana, he saved me."

"Saved you from what?"

Chakotra relieved Haana and pulled herself back, opened her towel that was wrapped around her head, opened her hair just like a hot heroine from Mahesh Bhatt's movie.

"What a man he is? A real man, I must say."

"I am not getting you, aunty, kindly explain how come you came here on a stretcher, Sikander? What all are you talking about!"

"I went swimming, however, I was standing by the pool in my sexy swimsuit, when I saw Sikander coming and sitting on the chair bare-chested. I can't tell you how sexy his physique is. I was looking at him when I don't know how my legs slipped and I fell into the pool and the water was also deep. To take advantage of the situation, I called out his name, he too jumped into the pool and saved me, I pretended to be unconscious, He lifted me in his arms and took me out of the pool."

'Is he alive?"

Fortunately, Chakotra was too excited and lost in explaining the moments that she did not hear it.

"How safe I felt in his arms, what fragrance? Wow Haana, I felt like a 16-year-old. He dived into the pool, lifted me, my body touched his chest, then he gently kept me like Mumtaz on the sofa at the reception. He should be named as Shah Jahan than Sikander."

Haana looked at Chakotra in jealousy. A 23-year-old should enjoy these moments with him rather women double her age, telling her how much fun she had with her crush. Life was unfair.

"Are you okay now? Haana asked unbothered.

"Oh yes! The comfort he gave me had no room for pain. Sikanderrrr, umuahhhhh…"

Haana's eyes were wide open.

29

The Only Conversation & Last Meeting

SATURDAY 2 PM: PUBLISHER'S OFFICE

Haana visited her publisher's office where she was called for the contract signing. Haana went at the reception, where she was directed towards the publishing manager's office. Haana followed and knocked on the door of Shekhar's cabin. She was welcomed by Shekhar when she saw Shekhar and Sikander talking to each other. Shekhar asked Haana to sit and asked the duo to excuse him for a while.

Pin drop silence in the room, Sikander and Haana were sitting next to each other.

Haana's received a message from Chakotra saying, "Don't worry about me dear, I am leaving for Mumbai Darshan, I will see the city and will be back before night, never know I might see my BADSHAH too."

After five minutes, Sikander pulled his chair and took the paperweight in his hand to hide his nervousness,

"Can I help you anyway with your book?" Sikander asked.

For the first time, they both exchanged words.

Haana did not look at him, smiled and said: "Read it."

Shekhar entered, shook hands with Sikander and went to see him off.

Another message on WhatsApp

2:15 pm: Chakotra's selfie in front of Mannat.

2:30 pm: Juhu beach in a big gown with a hat and yellow glasses on her face

3:00 pm: Jalsa

Haana was disturbed now and then, she muted the conversation.

Shekhar came in and they proceeded with their meeting, the contract signing formality. It took all day for Haana to discuss the finest things of her book, royalty calculation, copyright, editing, distribution etc.

Same Day: 7 pm

Haana came back to her hotel, took the keys from the reception and proceeded towards her room. Where she saw Sikander's room opened and was being cleaned. She enquired the room service cleaning the room, he informed,

"The visitors would check in tomorrow so we are cleaning the room."

"Visitors? But someone else was already in? Haana confirmed.

"Yes! Ma'am, Sir has left."

"When?"

"5 minutes before."

"Ohkeyyyy" Haana answered.

She hurriedly opened her room and went to the window, pulled the curtains and saw Sikander standing next to his car with two men who came to drop him- as per Haana's assumptions. Sikander talked to them for five minutes, Haana looked at him like an admirer, tears came to her eyes, her face became no different from a 7-year-old who failed to get what she wants. Sikander shook hands with them, looked straight away at Haana's window as if he already knew she was standing, they both looked at each other. Somewhere they knew that it was their last meeting,

107

they knew their story would end there. Sikander stared for quite a few seconds as if he wanted to capture Haana's image in his mind if not heart for the last time. He too had no expression on his face. He turned back and sat in his car and left for the airport. Haana looked at him without a blink and continued till the car went far became small, smaller and finally disappeared. The last two tears from Haana's eyes felt for Sikander.

30

A New Outlook towards Life & People

The next morning Haana and Chakotra had to leave back for Delhi. Haana was keeping her things in the handbag. Chakotra stood before the beautiful glass window that showed the outside view, it was a 5-star hotel, the one standing at the window can see the whole campus of the hotel, the swimming pool, the greenery, the wide beautiful sky. That was the place where Haana and Sikander silently waved goodbye to each other. However, Haana never saw Pummy aunty for some time. When she took note of her, she realised that she was in some deep thinking.

"Anything interesting outside?"

No answer, the silence took over deep.

Haana cleared her throat and asked again, "Something very interesting outside, Pummy Aunty?"

The lady made no movements, no answer.

Haana could see her from behind, breathing deeply with her one hand overlapped by the other, a very comfortable yet defensive posture.

Haana did not know what was wrong with her. However, that time she did not call her, rather she came out of the bed and went near Pummy Aunty and touched her on her shoulder. Pummy Aunty became conscious and looked at

Haana and smiled, and went back to look outside without retaining eye contact with Haana, who kept on looking at her, noticing her pale and dry face. Her eyes were filled with tears with no makeup at all. She looked indifferent, never like before. Not because she was not in the makeup but because there was something genuinely wrong with her. Haana had seen Pummy aunty without makeup several times before but for the first time, Haana couldn't make out what was so different?

She looked at her eyes to see what was she looking at. She saw her looking at the two children swimming at the pool. Then she realised what might have made her sad. She did not utter a word and she had no idea how she could console the 42-year-old lady on something that she was even unsure to talk about.

"I am very happy for you," she said in a soft voice without making eye contact.

Haana did not understand and looked at her. She looked at Haana back and said,

"I am happy for you beta but more for your family that how happy and proud they would feel once you become an author. Doing everything for your kids for years and then one day seeing them doing things for themselves is what makes a parent feel accomplished, for they know that now their kids are grown up. You chased your passion and still, you are pursuing it and once you become a successful author, it wouldn't only be you who would be successful but your parents too, for now, they know that. *The seed planted by them is ready to provide shelter to so many.* However, I am deprived of this privilege. The lord did not find me capable to invest emotionally on my kid. I couldn't plant any seed; however, he has given me everything else and I am grateful for all those blessings. I have a husband who loves me and gives me all the freedom to do whatever I want to do."

She closed her eyes, took a deep breath and continued "I have no complaints, I am grateful for everything."

#

Haana did not know how life had changed her. Last night she lost SIKANDER forever, and then she discovered that face of Pummy aunty. What not she thought of her? Haana had a deep regret that she thought of Pummy aunty as Chakotra, a lady that sucks, a 42-year-old who went bananas over her crush, flirted with him, went for Mumbai Darshan all alone, but they were only a way to divert her mind from her loneliness. Haana realised how wrong she was, how unfair she had been. She finally was thankful to the Universe for that trip and especially with Pummy aunty, as she not only met with Sikander but also understood the reason why people react to situations in a certain way.

She did not want Pummy aunty to behave in a way that she did but still, it was her reason to do so. If Pummy aunty wouldn't have done things that she had, she would have probably gone into depression, so to avoid that she wore a mask on her face as a barren lady who was still happy and full of life, when deep inside only she knew how incomplete she was. Similarly, she wanted Sikander to propose her, confess his feelings but he didn't, though she knew he liked her back because he couldn't react in the way that Haana wanted him to.

Haana realised *'He didn't just have a physique of IRON, But a Heart of GOLD'*

That trip gave her a different and better perception towards people and situation. Haana finally knew it was 'her destiny' that made everything happened the way it did.

Haana's book was launched 15 days back. She was in an event for her book signing, when she received **AN UNEXPECTED NOTIFICATION:**

Hi Haana,

I have no words to describe what you have done because you already know. I feel ten times more popular now :D as you have mentioned "a social media swagger." I would like to congratulate you on your book. My condition was no different from you when I read the book. I felt so cold. I didn't know I made you go through these things all these times. You made me a character, an eternal character. I feel so powerful as a person. I feel much stronger than before. You have changed the definition of love, at least what I knew until I read the book. I didn't know one can admire the other person so much that their love towards them can make them a strong and better person. I believed love make us weak, our dependency on the other person makes us lose ourselves but I didn't know I acted as a light for you that now you can enlighten so many other people's lives through your words. Yes! I gave you mixed signals because I liked you but a promise made to another person could not be broken. We are humans we make mistakes; we love someone and get attracted towards someone else but trust me you were not merely an attraction, but that doesn't mean I don't love my girl: of course I do and that's what bound me in confessing my feeling towards you. But I love you in a way that is pure & respectful. You have taught me that love doesn't only mean 'being together' but also 'being patient' towards each other, waiting for the other person without knowing whether they would ever return to you or not. I still remember the day I saw you for the first time in the cafe and now that you are a successful writer, I can witness the change-the transformation from a girl to a lady. I feel honoured that I could be the reason behind someone's transformation.

Thank You for setting an example that if two person can't be together, they can not only curse, cry and moan but also they can be independent, strong and happy. You are full in yourself; you don't need anyone to complete you as much as I know you (stalking from far.) You dare to ask for what you want and yes you got it if not me this time but a thing far better than me i.e. your purpose, your true calling.

Your Social Media Crush,
Mr Muscle (Sikander)

She never confessed; He never proposed.

Yet, he became her biggest Lie,

and she became his most beautiful secret.